SECRETS

Love, Betrayal, and Revenge

NEVER DIE

EYONE WILLIAMS

National Best Selling Author of Lorton Legends

Secrets Never Die

BY

EYONE WILLIAMS

www.dcbookdiva.com

Scan and follow us everywhere!

ISBN-10: 098461107x
ISBN-13: 9780984611072
Library of Congress Control Number:

Paperback Edition, April 2012

Publisher's Note

This is a work of fiction. Any names historical events, real people, living and dead, or the locales are intended only to give the fiction a setting in historic reality. Other names, characters, places, businesses and incidents are either the product of the author's imagination or are used fictiously, and their resemblance, if any, to real life counterparts is entirely coincidental.

Edited by: Jenell Talley
Inside Layout: Linda Williams

DC Bookdiva Publications
#245 4401-A Connecticut Ave
NW, Washington, DC 20008
www.dcbookdiva.com
facebook.com/thedcbookdiva
twitter.com/dcbookdiva

Dark Secrets Begin

"Who did it, Niya? Who pulled the trigger?"

I rolled my eyes at the detective and sighed. He was getting on my fucking nerves asking me the same damn question in different ways after I had already told him I ain't know shit about the murder in front of my apartment building. So what I saw the whole thing go down? Shit like that went down all the time in my hood. It wasn't any of my business, and the streets of D.C. had schooled me well—I knew how to mind my damn business. I had seen too many people who opened their mouth about something that had nothing to do with them turn up missing.

The white detective glared at me and said, "What if that was your brother or cousin out there dead, for no reason? Would you still know nothing, as you say, young lady?"

I yawned, tired from hanging out all night at the go-go. "I can't tell you what I don't know. Sorry." I shrugged. I was ready to get the fuck on about my business.

The detective sighed with frustration. He shook his head knowing he was going to get no info out of me. "Come on, I know somebody outside saw something. Nobody can keep a secret in the streets."

Pissed off, I sucked my teeth and said, "Look, man, I don't know shit. I ain't see shit. How many times I gotta tell you that?" I shook my head and looked at my Gucci watch. It was 2:37 p.m. It was definitely time to roll.

Fed up, the detective walked over to the thick wooden door, opened it, and said, "I'm done for now. You can go."

He ain't have to tell me twice. I was out of there.

Once downstairs, I called my sister Jasmine and asked her to come get me from the police headquarters, where the homicide branch was located. Jasmine told me she was on her way. I shut my phone and sighed. Jasmine was always there for me, like Johnnie-on-the-spot.

Jasmine was my heart. At 25, she was seven years older than I was. However, she had been my sister/guardian since I was 14. On the real, she raised me. Our mother was sentenced to twenty-two years in federal prison in 2002 for serving an undercover one hundred and fifty grams of crack. Our father was a street legend in D.C., or so I was told. He came up with the likes of Michael "Fray" Salters and Eddie Mathis. I had heard so many stories about my father, Marvin Truman. He was shot to death in 1991, when I was only 5 years old. I never got over that. Nevertheless, life goes on. Moms held it down like a true soldier, doing whatever she had to do. Back then I didn't know that meant moving coke to take care of me and Jasmine, until I saw it on the news after the feds raided our Silver Spring, Maryland, home. Shit really hit the fan after that. Moms was sent off to federal prison. The feds took everything we had. Me and Jasmine moved back to the hood, our real home—uptown D.C. We had lived everywhere: Garfield Terrace, 10th and W, Kennedy Street, and Georgia Avenue. We got an apartment on Georgia Avenue and Rittenhouse Street, in Northwest. From then on, Jasmine made sure we were well taken care of—by any means.

A short while later, Jasmine pulled up in her white Range Rover. She sat behind the wheel in a pair of black Prada shades, fly as shit. As always, her hair was freshly done and her gear was top of the line: Gucci this, Fendi that. Her cute face and golden-brown skin looked just like mine—we got it from moms.

I jumped in the Range, and we pulled off into traffic. It was warm outside, so I put the window down and let the wind blow in my face for a second.

Moving through traffic, Jasmine said, "So what was they asking you up in there?"

"Regular bullshit—who did it, what did I see, and all that." I looked down at my vibrating cell phone and saw that it was this dude named Face. He was cool, but I decided to call him back later. Didn't really feel like talking.

Heading up 7th Street, Jasmine asked, "What did you tell them peoples?"

"I told them I ain't know shit. What else was I gon' tell them?" I said that with a little attitude. Jasmine knew me better than to ask me some shit like that. I ain't fuck with no cops.

My sister smiled at my response. "Did they bring up Jay's name?"

"Nah, they ain't bring up his name at all."

Jay was the one who really did the killing the cops were asking me about. Talk had it that Jay smoked this dude named Tyriq because Tyriq kicked in the door of his apartment and stole $50,000. By the way, Jay was also my sister's man. He was well respected in the streets of D.C. He was cool as shit, and. I had a lot of love for him. On top of that, my mother used to deal with him way back in the day, so it made him cool long before he started messing with Jasmine. On everything, Jay was a fly nigga, a real uptown nigga who was about his paper. And he was willing to do everything in his power to protect it. He was dangerous. He would smoke a nigga in the blink of an eye, like it wasn't shit.

"Niggaz ain't crazy," I said. "Ain't nobody gon' say shit about him to the police."

Jasmine sighed. "Don't believe that. Niggaz out here are snakes—they'll tell on they mother to get out of going to prison."

I laughed. "Ain't that the truth."

Jasmine smirked, "Yeah, but he ain't to be fucked with."

Her phone rang. She checked the number and answered it. From the sound of the conversation, I could it was Jay. She was telling him about my visit to the homicide branch. Her conversation with him was short and sweet. She ended the call with him, looked at me,

and said, "Jay said you did good, said you a good girl."
She winked at me and laughed.

I rolled my eyes and blushed. Growing up, I had
a little crush on Jay's fine ass, but I would never cross my
sister like that and fuck her man. That wasn't in my
blood. Blood was always thicker than water. That's how
my mother raised us.

"I hope the police don't keep pressin' me 'bout
that shit."

"Don't worry about it, Niya. They'll be
investigating another murder in a day or two. Don't even
trip. Shit will blow over. Plus, you wasn't the only one
outside that night."

Her words comforted me. She'd had that kind of
effect on me ever since I was a little girl.

As if I didn't know any better, Jasmine said,
"Niya, I don't want you talkin' to nobody about that shit
that went down. Okay?"

I sucked my teeth and caught a little attitude
about that shit. "Come on, Jaz, you know damn well I
know how to keep my mouth shut. Miss me with that
bullshit. I ain't no little girl."

Jasmine laughed. "My bad. Oh, I forgot you 18
now. You all grown up now."

I couldn't be mad at her for joking about my age;
in reality, she had treated me like I was grown since I
was, like, 14. Coming up, she let me learn on my own,
but she still made sure she taught me how shit really
went too. She taught me how to be tough, take care of
myself, how to recognize game niggaz spit, how to
survive in the mean streets, and how to never let a

motherfucker get out on me. Moms had taught her the same shit.

"Niya, who all was outside when Tyriq got shot?"

I told Jasmine it was me, two of my girlfriends, and a few niggaz from around the way. I named them all. I was sure she would pass the information on to Jay for safe keeping.

We pulled up in front of our building on Rittenhouse Street. A few street dudes were standing across the street by the alley doing their thing. Hustling was all they knew. Me and Jasmine were always safe and comfortable around the way. Everybody knew us; we were like family to them. Jasmine parked behind Jay's royal-blue Bentley GT. Jay was leaning against the car smoking weed and talking on his cell phone. He had on a white T-shirt, blue jeans, and black Jordans. The diamonds in his chain and the big one in his pinky ring stood out, making it clear that he was getting more money than most niggaz on the block. He had sexy, smooth dark skin—that shit that drove the ladies crazy in the streets. When he smiled, his bright white teeth made him look even finer. He kept his hair cut low, with thick waves. His swagger was full-blown. His right-hand man, Troy, was sitting inside the Bentley counting money. A few dudes who looked up to Jay were nearby. Everybody loved being around Jay.

Jay ended his call and smiled at me as I stepped out of the Range. I was looking good as shit in my Seven jeans. I nodded at Jay and said, "What's up?"

He slipped his phone in his pocket and went in his other pocket and pulled out a handful of fifties and hundreds—all big faces. He handed me damn near a thousand and said, "Here, Niya, take this and hit the mall. Treat yourself, baby girl. I fucks with you; I like how you keep your mouth closed." He winked.

"You know what it is," I smiled. "I mind my business. Good lookin', though." I stuffed the money in my Gucci bag. That was my reward for not saying a word to the police about what I saw.

Jasmine came around the truck with her arms folded. The look on her face made it clear that she had an attitude with Jay, which was wild because she was just talking to him like everything was all good. I figured that the attitude must have been about some shit from earlier. That was none of my business.

Jay looked at Jasmine and smiled. "Why you actin' like that, boo?"

"Don't 'boo' me, nigga." Jasmine rolled her eyes and shifted all of her weight to her right leg, looking real hood.

I started to wonder what was up with them. They didn't do too much beefin'.

Jay slid up on Jasmine real smooth, put his arm around her, and walked her down the block as they talked about whatever was going on.

While that was going down, Troy stepped out of the Bentley and lit a fat-ass Backwood. He took a long pull and blew smoke in the air.

He reminded me of 50 Cent. He was handsome and had the body of a nigga who just came home from prison. One of those niggaz who spent all his time doing push-ups and pull-ups on the inside. He undressed me with his eyes and said, "Damn, Niya, you up in them jeans, baby."

He always flirted with me.

I rolled my eyes and gave him a look like, Whatever, nigga! I couldn't fake, though—I loved the attention from him. But I couldn't be just another piece of pussy to him. If he wanted to get between my legs, it was going to take more than that bullshit he was spittin'. He'd only been home from prison a few months, so I knew he was trying to fuck everything he saw. When he went to prison I was 13, so it was understood that at 18, I was a whole new Niya, with everything in the right places body-wise.

Walking up on me, Troy said, "I see you all grown up now … lookin' good as shit." He smiled, then licked his lips.

I looked him up and down, put my hand on my hip, and said, "You tell everybody that, don't you?" I thought back to when he used to give me money for the ice cream truck. Now he was trying to fuck me. Niggaz!

"Nah, I don't tell everybody that, but I'm tellin' you that, baby. You a grown woman now from what I can see." He leaned to his left, then his right, looking at my thick hips and thighs.

I tried hard not to blush, but the nigga was laying it on thick.

Troy looked around at the young niggaz on the block and said, "Which one of these young niggaz you fuckin' wit' out here?"

I rolled my eyes and sucked my teeth. "I told you I ain't fuckin' wit' nobody right now," I said, snaking my neck. "Niggaz on some bullshit out here. I got a few friends, though."

Troy licked his lips and said, "Fuck friends. You need a man. I'll do somethin' big wit' your lil' sexy ass. I'll eat that pussy and all that, baby."

I smiled. That made my pussy wet. With the lips he had, I was sure he could eat some pussy like a real pro, but I had to pass. I waved his ass off and said, "Nigga, please, I ain't fuckin' wit' your ass." I stepped off. I could feel his eyes all over me, glued to my ass. I looked back and he was stuck, shaking his head like, Damn, I'll burn her little ass up. I winked at him and headed inside my building.

Jasmine came in behind me. From the look on her face, it seemed like things were cool with her and Jay. I said, "You cool?"

"Yeah, I'm good. Jay just be on some bullshit sometimes."

"You love 'em, though."

"Yeah, I do, but that don't mean he don't get on my damn nerves sometimes."

We made our way inside the apartment. I sat on the sofa and turned on the TV, straight to BET. Jasmine got on the computer and started checking her Facebook page.

"Niggaz always think they slick," she said, eyeing a picture of some girl. "They be too smart for their own good. They be so smart they dumb sometimes. Jay fuckin' this bitch Tish and keep talkin' 'bout it's business and shit, like I'm dumb. He got her makin' runs for him and shit, but ain't no bitch gon' be runnin' around for a nigga that ain't givin' her no money or no dick. I can read between the fuckin' lines."

I got up and went over to the computer to check out the girl. Tish was wearing next to nothing on her Facebook page.

"Oh, that bitch Tish doin' way too much on there." I watched as Jasmine went through Tish's pictures. "Jay fuckin' *her?!*" I asked.

Jasmine "Yeah, Jay fuckin' her, wit' his bitch ass. I don't know what kinda fool he think I am. I know how the game go. I just play along with the shit."

"I'll beat that bitch's ass for you when I see her. She ain't shit."

Jasmine laughed. "Don't trip. I got it under control, boo. But trust and believe Jay ain't the only one that can play that game." She shook her head. "I ain't even gon' trip. Jay pay our rent, he pay the car note on my Range, and he keep me fresh. I stay diggin' in them pockets. Pretty soon we gon' have our own house, and we ain't gon' have to worry about none of these no-good-ass niggaz out here."

I smiled. Jasmine knew how to get what she wanted in life, and I admired that.

Her cell phone rang. She answered it. "Yeah ... okay ... I'ma do it right now. I'll call you when I'm done."

She got up, went to her room, and returned with a brown shopping bag. She set the shopping bag on the kitchen counter. She pulled out a pot and some baking soda, put some water in the pot, and sat it on the stove. She cut the fire on and put some heat under the pot. I was paying close attention. She pulled a brick of powder coke out the shopping bag, cut the wrapper with a knife, and dumped the coke in the pot. After mixing a little baking soda into the pot, she began to work her magic. Our mother taught her how to whip powder into hard white. If the coke was good, Jasmine could turn two bricks of coke into three like it wasn't shit. She had a nice little hustle: She charged $1,000 to turn two bricks into three. A few dudes around the way were moving weight in the coke game but couldn't whip like Jasmine, so they stepped to her to get their shit right.

I watched her work. Even though I didn't fuck around with that shit, I had watched her do her thing long enough to know how to do it myself.

"Jaz, you make that shit look so easy, like you been doin' it all your life," I said.

She laughed. "Ain't shit to it. I been doin' it since I was 'bout 14." She continued to whip the coke with a fork like it was cake batter. "So what's up wit' Troy? I see he been pushin' up on you jive hard."

I rolled my eyes and smirked. "I ain't thinkin' 'bout no damn Troy. He just want some pussy. How old is he anyway?"

"He a year or two older than Jay, so he gotta be 26 or 27. Somethin' like that. He on the come-up, though. If you work your shit, you could have that nigga eatin' out the palm of your hand. You know how the game go, girl."

"Eatin' out the palm of my hand, huh?" I smiled, thinking about how Troy said he'd eat my pussy. Being so much older, I was sure he could suck my pussy dry. That turned me on. No bullshit! "Troy been comin' at me real hard, talkin' that pussy-eatin' shit."

Jasmine smiled and shook her head. "Yeah, Niya, you got his attention. Make that nigga chase you, baby girl. You throw that young pussy on 'em, and he won't know what to do. He just got out too."

I laughed and changed the subject. "We still goin' to see Ma this weekend?"

"Yeah, I hope so," Jasmine said as she finished cooking the first brick. She set it on a plate and put the other one in the pot.

Thinking about my mother made me miss her. We hadn't been to visit her in close to two months. Every time we turned around something new popped up, and we couldn't make it up the road to West Virginia to visit her at Alderson. Still, we stayed in touch with her and took good care of her. Jasmine made sure she did all she could for our mother. Moms wanted for nothing while she did her time.

As the years passed, I grew used to the fact that she was going to be away for a while. I just prayed that she wouldn't have to do the whole twenty-two years the judge gave her. I also grew to hate the system for giving her so much fucking time. Shit, I knew niggaz doing tens and fifteens for smoking niggaz in the streets, but my moms was sitting in on twenty-two years for crack. Bullshit! For real. I had cried myself to sleep so many nights when she first got sentenced. But at the end of the day, it was nothing I could do about the situation but suck it up and be strong. That's the way moms wanted me to be.

There was nothing I wouldn't give to have my moms back in the free world with us. Shit just wasn't the same without her. And all the visits, letters, phone calls, and pictures would never add up to having her free, back with us.

"Ay, Jaz," I said, "I need to get those pictures developed for Ma. I keep forgetting to do it."

Jaz smirked while she was hard at work over the stove. "Not you, Ms. Always On Top of Business."

I laughed. "Shut up, ho. I'ma do it right now, right this minute while we talkin' 'bout it. Let me see your keys."

Jazmin gave me a serious look and said, "Niya, go to the store and bring my shit right back. Don't be all over the city in my shit, showin' off. You know how you get."

I sucked my teeth. "Whatever." Grabbing the keys to the Range off the coffee table, I said, "Ease up, Jaz. I got you. I'll be right back."

I went to my room, grabbed my digital camera, and hit the door.

* * *

I hit CVS to get the pictures developed, and then I hit McDonald's to grab something to eat real quick for me and Jasmine. I heard someone call my name as I walked back to the truck carrying my food. I turned around and saw Face. He was coming across the parking lot on a mountain bike.

Face was my age, but he acted much older. He was one of the few young niggaz who really had something on his mind and wanted to be more than just a street nigga. He was from 14th Street. His dark skin always attracted me to him. So did his bright smile. And his well-kept dreads that came down to his shoulders. He was tall, dark, and handsome. He could use a little meat on his bones, but he was still sexy to me. However,

I wasn't really taking him seriously, even though he was coming at me hard every chance he got. I finally gave him my number a few days prior.

"Niya, what's up, sexy?" Face said, stopping his bike right beside me.

I smiled and set my food on the hood of the Range. "I'm good. What's up with you?"

"I'm good, but I could be a lot better if you gave a nigga some play. Feel me?"

I blushed as I looked him in the eyes, noticing how pretty his brown eyes were. His outfit was cool too. He was rocking a purple and black short sleeve Polo shirt, blue jeans, and a pair of black and purple Jordans. The more I thought about it, the more I could see myself giving Face some play, maybe even some pussy if he acted right. I wasn't really trippin' off the fact that he was riding a bike. Shit, I understood his pain—he wasn't selling drugs; he had a nice little job at Howard University in the mail room. At least if I did get into a relationship with him I wouldn't have to worry about him going to jail. Fuck all that shit.

Face said, "I see you blushin'. Yeah, that's right, let me see that smile."

"Stop it," I said. I couldn't help but laugh.

He glanced at the Range Rover. "I see you ridin' in style."

"My sister let me push it to run to the store. You know she ain't gon' let a bitch go too far in her pride and joy. Shit, I wish it was mine."

He nodded. "I feel you. So other than that, what's up wit' you? Why you been duckin' my calls?"

"Don't take it like that. I was kinda caught up in some serious shit. I was gon' hit you back a little later on, see what you was up to."

He looked at me like, Yeah, right.

I laughed at the look he gave me. "For real, I was, Face. Believe that."

"Okay, if you say so. I'ma take your word for it. I'm not gon' hold you up, though, so just call me later. Cool?"

"I will, I promise." I winked.

He smiled and rode off, heading up Georgia Avenue.

I jumped in the Range and headed home.

* * *

Later on, I sat in my bedroom on the computer checking out Face's Facebook page. He was into music real heavy. He made beats, hip-hop joints. I listened to a few of his beats and found myself nodding my head. He was tight. His beats had a down-South feel to them mixed with a little D.C. flavor—a touch of go-go. There were two songs on there that he produced for Karim Mowatt's Gunplay Records and another he produced for Cinquan's Real Live Records. His Facebook page said that he was an aspiring producer with dreams of putting D.C. on the map for real. His Facebook status read: "I make beats that real niggaz rap to!" I smiled. I thought that was cute. There were tons of pictures of him on his page. He had pictures with Tabi Bonney, Wale, and a few other rappers from the D.C. area. Face was getting more interesting by the minute.

I grabbed my cell phone and called him.

"It must be my lucky night," he said as he answered the phone. I could hear a loud beat playing in the background, a joint that I could picture a Lil Wayne or a Young Jeezy rapping over.

I laughed and in true diva form said, "Yeah, it's your lucky night. Any night I call you is your lucky night."

"I hear that, but if it was really my lucky night you would be over here wit' me." He killed the music in the background.

"Yeah, whatever."

"What's up, though? What you up to?"

"Sittin' in my room lookin' at your Facebook page. I see you got some stuff goin' on. I like that."

"I try," he said.

"That's right. I like that."

"I like you." He made it clear that he was flirting. I smiled.

A knock on my bedroom door grabbed my attention. It was Jasmine. I put Face on hold for a second and told my sister to come in.

"Niya, I'm 'bout to go out for a little while. I'll catch you later. Call me if you need anything, okay?"

"Okay, see you when you get back."

"Love ya."

"Love you too," I said.

Jasmine left, shutting my door behind her.

Turning my attention back to Face, I said, "So you really into this music thing, huh? You serious about it, I see."

"Yeah, I ain't playin'. It's my dream. I put my all into it, Niya."

"I respect that," I said. "So you sell your beats?"

"Yeah, but I don't have a big name, so I only get a few dollars for them right now. Only local artists support me right now. I get a few hundred dollars here and there. Maybe a thousand if I'm lucky. Nothin' much right now. I gotta pay my dues, but it will pay off sooner or later, so I can't complain."

I nodded. "I understand. That makes sense."

Gunfire went off outside. Sounded like ten or fifteen shots. It made me jump. It was so loud it sounded like it was right in my bedroom. Seconds later, I heard a car horn blaring nonstop.

Face said, "Gotdamn, fuck is goin' on over there?"

"You heard that?" I said.

"Hell yeah. Sounded like that shit was right in the room wit' you."

"That shit scared the shit out of me. Somebody musta got they ass tore up out there," I said. The sound of gunshots around my way was no big deal.

The car horn kept blaring. Somebody had gotten fucked around real bad, I could tell.

Moments later I heard banging at my front door. *Who the hell is banging on my damn door like that?* I thought. "Ay, Face, let me call you back in a second," I said as I headed to the front door.

"Okay, make sure you hit me back," he said.

"I will."

I got to the door and looked out the peephole. It was Ms. Mary, my neighbor, an older woman who used to babysit me when I was a little girl. I opened the door without hesitation.

Ms. Mary was hysterical. "Oh, my God, baby ... Jasmine ... Jasmine ... Jasmine ..."

She kept saying my sister's name over and over again.

My heart began to pound in my chest. I experienced a fear like nothing I had ever felt in my life. "Jasmine what, Ms. Mary? What about my sister?"

"They shot her! They shot her! Somebody shot her!"

My heart dropped. My knees got weak. I got light-headed. Time seemed to stand still. For a second, I couldn't even speak; words wouldn't come out of my mouth. I shook my head like what she was saying wasn't true. She couldn't know what she was talking about. She had to be mistaken.

"No, no, you don't know what you are talkin' about. You can't be right." I shook my head in disbelief. Tears began to pour from my eyes as the thought of what she was saying hit me. "Nooooooo, nooooooo, noooooo!" I screamed.

Ms. Mary was crying as well. My legs gave out and I would have hit the ground if it wasn't for Ms. Mary catching me. She grabbed me and held me tightly.

"Oh, baby, I'm so sorry," she sobbed.

I snatched away from her and ran downstairs to see what the hell was going on outside.

* * *

The police were all over the place. Red and blue flashing lights filled Rittenhouse Street. It was as if JFK had been assassinated on my block. Jasmine's Range Rover was surrounded by cops. She was still inside slumped forward with her head on the wheel. The horn was still blaring. A crowd of people was gathering around, trying to find out what was going on. The driver's door of the Range had bullet holes in it. The window was shot out. Brains were all over the windshield. I couldn't stand seeing my sister like that. I didn't know if I was going to pass out or throw up. I got dizzy for a second but managed to run toward the Range. I had to get close to my sister. "Noooooo!" I yelled as I tried to run through the sea of police officers. "That's my sister!" I screamed and sobbed. An officer grabbed me. I struggled with him. It took two of them to restrain me. "That's my sister, noooooooooo, that's my sister!"

<u>Who Can I Trust?</u>

Inside my apartment, Jay held me tightly as I cried on his shoulder. We were sitting on the sofa in the living room. I was crushed, my whole world had been torn apart in a matter of moments.

Rubbing my arm in a brotherly way, Jay said, "Let it all out. I understand, I understand." Jay was much stronger than I was, but he had tears in his eyes as well. He swore that whoever killed Jasmine would pay dearly. He tried his best to console me, but it was no use.

Thirty minutes earlier, homicide detectives had come to my apartment asking me a thousand questions. Questions I couldn't answer. And even if I could answer them, I didn't have the energy to do so. I was emotionally spent. I had just lost my only sister. I was now alone. All I had left was me. My father was dead, my mother was locked up, and now my sister was gone—murdered in cold blood. I couldn't even think straight. If the homicide detectives really understood what I was going through, as they said they did, then they wouldn't have wasted their time asking me all that bullshit. Who did I think would do something like that? Why would someone do something like that? Did Jasmine have any enemies? On and on with the bullshit. Even if I knew anything, I would only give those answers to Jay; I knew he would punish the motherfucker that murdered Jasmine.

I cannot express the pain I felt when they put that white sheet over Jasmine's body and hauled her off to the morgue. That was my flesh and blood, my only sister, the only person I could count on in these mean streets.

With my face buried in Jay's chest, I sobbed, "Why? Why would somebody do that? Why? For what?"

With a mask of anger on his face, Jay said, "I don't know, but I'ma find out. The streets talk. They always talk. I'm gon' get to the bottom of it. Believe that, Niya."

"What am I goin' to do without Jaz? I don't have nobody. I'm all by myself now." I sobbed harder as I thought about my situation.

"You'll get through this, Niya. I got your back. I'll make sure you okay." Jay continued to hold me tightly as he rubbed my arm, trying his best to comfort me. "I know it's hard for you, Niya. I feel your pain. I'm hurtin' too. You know how much I loved Jaz."

I was sobbing so hard that I began to block out all that Jay was saying. I began shaking like I was having a nervous breakdown. All I could feel was hopelessness, and that feeling covered me like a blanket. I didn't even want to live anymore, I didn't want to go on with life. I didn't know how I was going to tell my mother about Jasmine's death. The news was going to crush her. I didn't want her to have to deal with that in there. As I thought about my mother, I knew that I was all she had left. At that moment, I knew that I would have to find a way to remain strong. But how?

* * *

If it wasn't for Jay, I don't know how I would have made it through the days that followed Jasmine's murder. He took care of the funeral and paid for everything. He did it all as he dealt with her death in his own way, as street niggaz do. I could tell that her death was painful to him as well.

He wanted to be alone at the funeral. He didn't want anyone to see him cry. That wasn't a side he liked to show. Me, on the other hand, I couldn't stop crying. I couldn't eat, couldn't sleep, and wouldn't deal with anyone except Jay. I was turning to him for comfort and security. He understood exactly what I was going through. He would bring me food and make me eat. He took care of me. He assured me that I was not alone and that he had my back. I was grateful for that.

It was so hard to tell my moms what happened to Jasmine. It had to be one of the hardest things I've had to do in my whole life. When she called me, I told her what had happened as best as I could. She tried hard to be strong, but she broke down and sobbed on the phone. I had never heard so much pain in her voice. Not even when my father was murdered. I guess in some way she understood that since my father was in the game that death or prison came with that life. But her Jasmine was different. In my mother's eyes, she wasn't supposed to meet such a fate. One of the hardest parts of Jasmine's death for my moms was the fact that the prison didn't let her attend the funeral. That crushed her; she couldn't even see her baby off to the next life.

Days after Jasmine's funeral, Jay let me use her car to go visit my moms. I needed to see her so badly. I needed to hug her, kiss her, just be near to her. It only took a few hours to get to West Virginia. I used the time to clear my head and think about how I was going to take care of myself all by myself. Bills were already becoming an issue. Rent was due and that alone was stressing me being as though I didn't have a job.

In the visiting hall with my moms, I held myself together. I felt as though I had to for her sake. To my surprise, my moms was calm. She said that it was due to her faith in God. She looked like she was at peace with what had occurred. Nevertheless, I knew that a piece of my mother had died with Jasmine. It was no way around it.

"How are you holding up, Niya?" my moms asked, holding my hand.

I looked down at the floor for a second. "I'm takin' it one day at a time, Ma. That's all I can do, you know?"

She nodded understandingly. Gently, she touched my chin and turned my face to hers. "Listen to me, baby. You are strong. You are smart. Just like me. No matter what happens, you will make it. You hear me?"

I nodded. The tone of my mother's voice made me feel confident, at ease, like everything was going to be okay. I loved that about my mother. "I understand, Ma. I needed to hear that from you."

"I'm telling you how it is. Life must go on. You have to be strong. There's no other way to look at it," she said. "Life deals us hard blows at times. Stuff like this only makes us stronger. Only the strong survive. You know this."

She made so much sense. There was nothing we could do but mourn Jasmine and hold her memory in our hearts.

"Niya, you are all I have left, baby, all that keeps me going in here. I need you to be strong and keep your head up. Do whatever you have to do to make it. You are a grown woman now." Her eyes were so serious, but full of concern at the same time. She wanted her words to pierce my heart and sink into my mind. They did.

"I'm goin' to be okay. I'm goin' to be strong, Ma," I said. "I'll make it. Trust me. I just want to make sure you're okay in here."

She nodded a painful nod. "I've cried every night, cried my heart out about Jasmine, but that won't bring her back," she said shaking her head. "I worked so hard get us out of the 'hood, to get us away from what happens in the streets. I risked my life and my freedom for my family—you and Jasmine—to protect you both from the street life. Now I'm sitting here with all of this time and can't even help you get through these hard times. I couldn't even see my baby get laid to rest. I really feel like I let you both down."

"Don't do that to yourself, Ma. Ain't none of this your fault. You did your best. You did all you could do. You did what you had to do. You were always there for us, no matter what, even while you're in here."

My moms didn't say anything for a moment. I could tell she was in deep thought. She looked at me and said, "Have you heard anything about who killed Jasmine?"

I shook my head. "Don't nobody know much. Jay been lookin' into it."

My moms had watched Jay grow up. She knew what he was about. In fact, she'd fronted him his first brick when he first started moving weight. She used to say that he was going to be a major player in the game if he could stay alive—and free—long enough. I guess she saw something in him.

"What happened that night?" she asked.

I told her all I knew. According to what I'd gathered from Jay, Troy, and a few other people from around the way, a dude wearing all black and a ski mask ran up on the Range Rover and let off a rack of shots at close range. Bullets hit Jasmine in the head and chest.

Moms put her face in the palm of her hands and began to sob softly. I rubbed her back and began to cry again. The thought of what happened to my sister was too much to bare.

Moms looked up at me with tears in her eyes and said, "You tell Jay I said find out who killed my baby and tear their ass up! You hear me?! Tell him I said do their ass just like they did my baby!"

I nodded. "Jay told me he's goin' to do just that, Ma. He will, I know it. He will find out who killed Jaz. Watch."

We spent the rest of the visit comforting each other. When it was time to leave, I hugged my moms so tightly. I said, "I love you. I love you so much."

"Remember what I told you: Only the strong survive, Niya. You be strong out there and take care of yourself."

"I will, Ma."

"Go on now. I love you, baby," she said as she wiped tears from her eyes.

* * *

It took weeks, but I slowly began to accept life without Jasmine. Still, not a day went by that I didn't think about her. Living in the same apartment that I'd shared with Jasmine wouldn't allow me to move on completely. The only way to fully move on with my life was to get my own apartment. I needed a fresh start. In order to do that, I needed a job. I began to look for work. I was willing to work just about anywhere. Jay kept telling me that I didn't have to worry about getting a job and that he would look out for me, but I wanted to be able to look out for SELF. God bless the child that got her own. That's where my mind was. I got a job at Borders books in downtown D.C. The pay wasn't great, but it was a start. That's all I needed.

There was still no word about who killed Jasmine. All the dudes around the way had their ears to the street trying to find out who did the killing. It was a mystery to them and the police. I began to think that we would never find out who killed my sister.

Taking a little time out for myself, I sat on the sofa in my living room reading *Larceny* by Jason Poole. It was a D.C. story, one of those street novels. I had begun reading novels to clear my mind. Sometimes I would read the good ones in one day. As I read, there was a knock at the door. It spooked me a little. "Who is it?" I called out, sitting the novel on the coffee table as I got up.

"Jay."

I opened the door and let Jay in.

He rocked Gucci shades, a white T, a diamond chain, blue jeans, and black Jordans. He had a black Polo backpack in his hand.

"What's good, Niya? You okay?" he said as he shut the door.

"I'm good. What about you?" I said.

"I'm chillin'." He looked around. "It's so quiet in here. What you up in here doin'?"

"Readin'." I took a seat back on the sofa and picked up my novel. "I been doin' a lot of readin' lately. Helps me clear my mind."

"I feel you." Jay took a seat beside me. He sat the backpack on the floor by his feet. "I need you to hold this for me, Niya." He nodded toward the backpack.

I could pretty much tell what was inside: guns or drugs. On the real, I wanted nothing to do with that shit. However, Jay had done so much for me after Jasmine was murdered, I couldn't see myself telling him no about anything. I wouldn't feel right.

"What's in the bag?" I asked.

"Coke. Three bricks. Put it up for me. I'll get it from you later. Cool?"

Reluctantly, I said, "Okay, I got you, Jay."

"Good lookin', Niya. I fucks wit' you, baby girl." He rubbed my thigh. I was in a pair of tight-ass Seven jeans. Turning toward me, his face got dead serious, his eyes almost frightening. He said, "I got somethin' to tell you."

"What?"

"I know you know how to keep your mouth shut, so I'ma trust you wit' this, but you gotta promise me that you gon' take it to your grave wit' you, Niya."

My heart was pounding. Anxiety was running through my whole body like an injected drug.

Jay put his hand on my shoulder and said, "I found out who killed Jaz."

I couldn't believe it. I became enraged. "Who? Who did it?"

"You know the nigga Sean?"

"Yeah, I know him," I said.

Sean was a dude from W Street who paid Jasmine to whip coke for him. He also had a thing for her. Jay knew it.

"Word on the streets is that Jaz cooked up two bricks for Sean. She switched coke on 'em and gave him two and a half bricks of flower and B-12."

I snapped. "That's bullshit! Jaz wouldn't play no fuckin' games like that! You know she wouldn't do no shit like that!" I was beyond pissed off. I couldn't believe a nigga killed my sister for some bullshit like that.

"I know, I know, Niya," Jay said, trying to calm me down. "It don't even matter now. What's done is done. I got his bad ass, though. Trust and believe that, baby girl. I just wanted you and your mother to know I ain't bullshit on what I said I was gon' do. I ain't gon' let a nigga get away wit' no shit like that."

I hugged Jay. "Thank you, Jay. Make his ass pay for what he did to my sister."

Jay kissed my forehead softly. I felt so safe with him around. He hugged me tightly and rubbed my back. Then he got up. "I gotta roll out. I'ma take care of that nigga tonight. Just watch the news." He pointed at the backpack and said, "Put that up for me. Matter fact, you know how to cook that shit up like Jaz used to, right?"

"Yeah, it ain't nothin' to it," I said.

"Cool. Cook that shit and hold it for me."

"No problem. I got you," I said, grabbing the backpack.

Jay left.

I wasted no time cooking the coke into bricks of hard white, even added a little cut to stretch the work for him.

* * *

Later on, I was on the computer looking at Face's Facebook page. I really hadn't had much time for him since dealing with my sister's death. However, I did talk to him on the phone here and there. My mind just wasn't there to give him the kind of attention he wanted from me at the time. But he understood what I was going through, and I respected that. That made me look at him as a real friend. Sometimes he would just listen to what was on my mind, which made me feel like I had someone to talk to, and I needed that more than a boyfriend.

I grabbed my cell phone and called Face.

"What's up, Niya?" He sounded frustrated for some reason.

"I'm good. What's up wit' you? You sound like you got something on your mind."

He sighed. "Ain't nothin'. Just tryin' to make a few dollars the legal way, and shit ain't kickin' off the way I want it to."

I felt him on that. The little job I had was paying next to nothing; I was barely paying my rent on time. Jay had to throw me a few dollars for last month's rent.

"I know how you feel, Face. You just gotta hold on. Things will get better in due time, trust me on that. All your hard work will pay off. Stick to your game plan, believe in it, see it through."

"That's what I keep tellin' myself, but I can barely pay the rent. My moms just lost her job, and bills keep comin' in, one after another. Shit, it make a nigga wanna' hit the block."

I didn't like his frame of mind. I saw him as better than that, but what could I say to him? I was a firm believer in the saying "a man gotta do what a man gotta do."

"Face, I feel you. Believe me, I do, but at the same time you know that struggles come wit' everything in life. Hard times come and they go. Don't let hard times kill your dreams, boo. If you hit the block and get caught up, who's gon' be there to take care of your mother?"

"You know how to cheer a nigga up, don't you?"

"I'm just speakin' the truth. That's what a real friend is supposed to do."

Jay called on the other line. I told Face to hold on for a second.

"What's up, Jay?" I said when I clicked over.

"Ay, bring that backpack outside for me real quick."

"Okay, here I come."

"Good girl."

I clicked back over and said, "Face, I gotta take care of something real quick. I gotta hit you back, okay?"

"Cool. I'ma be waitin' for your call too."

I smiled. "Whatever," I joked. "For real, I'ma call you back in 'bout ten minutes."

I threw on my Prada tennis shoes, grabbed the backpack for Jay, and headed outside. My block was in full swing, even though it was close to midnight. Nightlife was a way of life on Rittenhouse Street. Jay was in his black Nissan 350 ZX. Troy was riding shotgun, talking on his cell phone. You rarely saw Jay without Troy. I walked up to the driver's side window. Jay lowered the window. Weed smoke came rushing out of the car. I handed Jay the backpack.

"I wrapped them up for you like Jaz used to."

Jay smiled as he looked in the backpack. "Good lookin' out, Niya." He looked me up and down in a way that I had never seen him do before. "You in them jeans, girl."

"Boy, please," I blushed.

He pulled a stack of bills from his pocket and handed them to me. "That's a G. I know your money funny right now, workin' that little job."

"Thanks, Jay," I said as I put the money in my pocket.

"Come here," he said, using his finger to signal me to lean inside the car. I did. He whispered in my ear, "Check out the newspaper tomorrow. I took care of that Sean situation. Touched 'em up real good too."

I wasn't really happy that someone was murdered, but I did feel as though whoever killed

Jasmine deserved to die, by all means. I was glad that Jay had issued street justice for my sister.

Jay whispered, "Take that to your grave, Niya." He winked.

"You know I will," I said as I stood up straight, feeling as though I was the only one who knew Jay's secret. It was yet another secret that he and I shared.

As I turned to walk away, Troy got off his cell phone, leaned across Jay, and said, "Damn, Niya, you can't speak?"

I smiled, rolled my eyes, and said, "You was all on the phone and shit, probably talkin' to one of your hoes. I ain't want to disturb you."

Troy smiled. "Yeah, whatever. You duckin' me. You know I'm tryin' to make you wifey."

I died laughing. Jay did too.

"Tell that shit to one of these young bitches that believe anything. I know all you wanna do is fuck. You just came home, nigga."

Troy laughed. "You gon' see — I'm get you before it's all over. I ain't gon' let one of these other niggaz get you."

"Whatever you say," I said with a smirk.

Jay cut in and said, "Don't pay him no attention, Niya."

I shook my head and said, "See y'all later. I'm gone."

Troy yelled out, "Ay, Niya, I'ma do something big wit' you, girl!"

I laughed to myself and kept walking. What Jay had just told me about Sean being dead was the only thing on my mind.

* * *

The next morning I went out and grabbed *The Washington Post*. I went straight to the Metro section and there it was:

> *A 22-year-old man was found slain in the 1500 block of 7th Street, Northwest. The victim has been identified as Sean Moore of the 2900 block of Georgia Avenue, Northwest. Around 9:15 p.m., yesterday, a gunman ran up to Moore's 2005 BMW SUV and opened fire with a semi-automatic handgun, striking Moore at least 13 times in the head, chest, and arm. Police say the murder appears to be drug related.*

When I was done reading about Sean's murder, I threw the paper in the trash. That was the end of that chapter of my life.

<u>Gotta Do What I Gotta Do</u>

Borders was busy. People had been in and out all day. The author/activist/hip-hop artist Sister Souljah was doing a book signing for her book *The Coldest Winter Ever.* The book was more than seven years old, but her loyal readers were still coming through to have copies of their books signed as if the book was brand new. I wasn't even hip to the book but decided to read it after I got a chance to speak to Sister Souljah for a second. She was so down to earth.

In the urban lit section, I was placing copies of Dutch's *Dynasty* on the shelf when I heard someone call my name. I turned around and smiled. It was my girl Lisa. Lisa was my girl from way back; we grew up together on Rittenhouse Street. I hadn't seen her since Jasmine's funeral.

I hugged her. "Girl, what's up?" I looked her up and down. She was fly as shit, as always. "I see you lookin' good."

She smiled. "It's an uptown thing. You know how we do it." We both laughed. "You not lookin' bad yourself."

"Shit ain't like it used to be, but I'm holdin' on," I said. "I can't complain, though."

Lisa nodded. "So how you been holdin' up?" she said as she picked up a copy of *Dynasty*.

"I'm okay, just tryin' to make ends meet. You see I'm workin' this little job. A bitch gotta eat."

She laughed. "I know that's right. I can't see it no other way. I gotta admit that I never thought I would see you doin' this 9-to-5 thing."

I shrugged. "It is what it is. I'm on my own now. I ain't got Jasmine to look out for me no more, so I gotta do what I gotta do. Ain't no gettin' around it."

"Jay don't be lookin' out for you?"

"Yeah, but that ain't my man. I can't call on him all the time, feel me?"

Lisa nodded. "I know that's right. I can't stand askin' a muthafucka for nothin'. I been like that since we was little. I'm go get it myself."

"Okay, now that's what I'm talkin' about," I said with a smile. "So what's new wit' you?"

"Girl, same ol' shit—stackin' this paper, tryin' to get out of that little-ass apartment. I be in the club until the sun come up, workin' them niggaz. You wouldn't believe how much paper them niggaz throw to see a phat ass or get a good lap dance."

"I feel you."

Lisa had been stripping for close to a year. She was making a killing doing it. She had the whole Alicia Keys look going on, and it drove niggaz crazy in the club. No matter what a motherfucker had to say about her, they had to respect her hustle. If it didn't make dollars, it didn't make sense to her. Simple as that.

I saw a copy of Sister Souljah's book in her Gucci bag and said, "I see you got that *Coldest Winter Ever* in your bag."

"I love Sister Souljah; *Coldest Winter Ever* was the first book I ever read. When I heard she was doin' a signin' here, I had to come through."

"That's what's up." I picked up the empty *Dynasty* box off the floor. I needed to get back to work. "Well, girl, I gotta to get back to work. I have a few things to take care of before closing. Call me later. Let's hook up, okay?"

"Okay, no problem. I'll hit you later. We can hit the club or something." She hugged me. "I love you, Niya."

"I love you too."

Lisa left and I got back to work.

Just before closing time my boss asked to speak with me in the back office. I went to see what he wanted. He looked uneasy, like something was wrong. Mr. Harris was a skinny white man with gray hair, and he wore thick glasses.

"Is something wrong, Mr. Harris?"

He sighed and rubbed his chin as if he was thinking of the best way to say what was on his mind. Avoiding eye contact with me, he said, "Niya, I like you. You come to work on time, you work hard, and you work well with the customers, but business is slow right now. My boss wants me to let two people go. I'm sorry ... I'm going to have to let you go, Niya."

"You're firing me?!" I couldn't believe my ears. I was in shock. He and I had just had a conversation about a promotion for me.

"It's out of my hands, Niya." He looked sad. "I'm really sorry. I truly am."

"You can't do this, Mr. Harris! I need this job! I really need this job!" I sounded desperate, and I felt like I was about to cry.

"It's nothing I can do about it, Niya."

I started to cry. Then I got angry and stormed out of the back room. I rushed out of the store without speaking to anyone. I sucked up my tears as I headed to the bus stop. I was sick of the hand life was dealing me. Life could be so unfair and unpredictable at times. I was mad at the world. Out of a job. Rent due. Refrigerator on E. I couldn't win for losing.

As I stood at the bus stop, a good-looking dude in a silver Benz pulled up and tried to holla at me. I was so mad I ignored his ass like he wasn't even there. I had no rap for anyone. He pulled off with a smug look on his face. I didn't give a fuck. He was about to get cussed the fuck out. My bus pulled up a few minutes later. I headed home wondering what the hell I was going to do next.

* * *

The next day I sat on the sofa in my living room in a pair of gray Polo sweats and a white T-shirt, telling Jay about losing my job. He listened as he rolled some loud in a Backwood. The TV was on BET; a T.I. video was on.

Jay lit the Backwood, took a few hits, and kicked his feet up on the coffee table like he was at home. Blowing smoke in the air, he said, "Fuck that job. You don't need no punk-ass job like that no way. It wasn't payin' you enough money anyway." He passed me the Backwood.

I hit it long and hard, held the smoke in my lungs as long as I could. It was too strong. I had a coughing fit.

Jay laughed. "Don't kill yourself, baby girl. Shit ain't that bad."

Still coughing, I said, "Fuck you, Jay" as I pounded my chest.

He continued to laugh.

I got myself together and said, "That job wasn't payin' shit no way—you right. But at the same time, it was better than nothin', Jay." I took another pull and blew smoke in the air.

"Niya, don't even worry about that job. I got you. You know that. I ain't gon' never see you do bad out here. Believe that." Jay grabbed the remote and put the TV on ESPN. He loved sports.

I was feeling what Jay was saying. It was all good. However, I didn't want him to take care of me. I wanted to take care of myself. Nevertheless, I was jobless. I knew I was going to have to put my pride to the side, at least for a hot second. Better days were sure to come.

I passed the Backwood back to Jay.

He hit it, took the smoke deep into his lungs and said, "I trust you, Niya, and bein' as though I trust you and fucks wit' you, I'ma always make sure you good. I got some shit in mind." He rubbed my thigh.

The smoke had me feeling nice; the shit was good.

Blowing smoke in the air, Jay said, "You ever been to New York?"

"Yeah," I nodded, "Jaz took me shoppin' up there a few times. Why?"

He passed the Backwood back to me and said, "I got a package that needs to be picked up, and I ain't got nobody I trust to go get it."

I felt uncomfortable. I said, "I thought you had your girl Tish for that?"

He smiled. "What you know about Tish?"

I hit the Backwood. "Come on, man, I ain't green at all. I'm hip to her. I know Jaz couldn't stand her ass, and I know I will beat that bitch's ass if she get in my business."

Jay laughed. "Yeah, well, with all that said, Tish is too emotional when it comes to me. I can't deal wit' that shit right now. It's gettin' in the way of gettin' money. I ain't got time for that shit."

"I see what you sayin'. She want you to be her man, and you ain't wit' it." I passed him the Backwood. I was good, didn't want any more. My eyes were half closed already.

"Yeah, she want more from me than I'm willin' to give. Losin' Jaz fucked me up real bad. I ain't got over it yet. Anyway, I cut Tish back."

I nodded. "So anyway, gettin' back to what you were sayin' about this New York thing—what's in it for me, Jay? Shit, after all, you askin' me to risk my freedom. That ain't no light thing there."

"I know, Niya, but you know where your ass at. You know how to watch your back. The shit ain't nothin'. I was payin' Tish $1,500, but for you, I'ma give you $2,000, off the top. Shit is simple—jump on the train to New York, meet my peoples, get the package, jump back on the train to D.C. You make two Gs just like that. How's that sound?"

"What if I get popped?"

"Don't even trip, Niya. It'll be your first charge. You'll be alright. If it was to go down, I'd get you right out, like clockwork. Anyway, as long as you follow directions, you'll be good. Tish did the same shit a thoudsand times over and never got popped. You way smarter than Tish. I know you can pull it off wit' no problem. Jasmine used to do it for me too, and she never got popped either. The shit is sweet, I'm tellin' you."

I laughed. "If it's so sweet, then why don't you make the trip yourself, huh?"

Jay smiled. "I like that about you, baby girl; you speak your mind. But to answer your question, I'm a felon two times over. If I get caught wit' some coke, I'ma fuck around and get life in prison. Shit just ain't sweet for me to be comin' back from New York wit' drugs on me. I look like a drug dealer. That's how the game goes."

"You got a point there." I laughed.

"So what's the deal? You down or what?"

I sighed. "Yeah, I'm down. How can I tell you no?" I winked.

"Good, girl. That's what's up." He smiled and rubbed my thigh. "I got you, believe that."

For some reason I loved when Jay said "good girl." I smiled.

"What you smilin' about?"

"Nothin'." I'd never tell him that I loved when he said that.

"Whatever. Anyway, I got a surprise for you."

"What?" I said excitedly, like a little kid.

"I got Jasmine's Range out the shop. It's just like new. I'ma let you hold it, okay?"

A smile big as Texas spread across my face. I was siced like shit! "For real, Jay?! Stop playin'!" I screamed, covering my mouth.

"I ain't playin, Niya." He pulled the keys out of his pocket and handed them to me.

He made my day. I didn't even care about losing my job anymore. "Thank you so much, Jay." I gave him a big hug.

* * *

A short while later I went to see Face. I knocked on his door. His mother answered. She was a short dark-skinned woman in her 50s. She had on a purple dress that looked like something she would wear to church. She looked very good for age. I could tell that she took good care of herself over the years.

"You're Niya, right?" she said with a smile. She let me into the apartment.

"Yes." I nodded politely, hopping I didn't smell like weed.

"You are such a pretty young lady. You look like … uh … what's her name? The singer girl …" She closed her eyes, searching for the name of the singer.

I smiled. I wanted to laugh.

"Rihanna! That's her name. You look like Rihanna, Niya." Looking me up and down she added, "You're a little thicker, but you still remind me of her." His mother was funny.

"People tell me that a lot," I said.

Face appeared from the back of the apartment. He looked good—sexy, in a street nigga way. His dreads were hanging down around his handsome face. He didn't have on a shirt. His skinny frame was cut up like he did a lot of working out; I could tell he did crunches and all that type of shit. He had a few tats. One on his chest said: Go Hard or Go Home. He had another across his stomach that looked like a money-counting machine with words around it that said: Money Makes the World Go Round. He folded his arms and smiled at me. *Damn.* That smile turned me on like shit.

"Gary, your friend Niya is so pretty," she said sweetly. I could tell I was going to like her.

Face nodded. "She is, isn't she, Ma? I have to agree with you. She could be a model or somethin'." He winked at me.

"I'll leave you two alone." She walked back to her room and shut the door behind her.

It was the first time I'd been inside Face's apartment. It was nice and clean, with a mother's touch.

I looked Face up and down, raised my eyebrow, and said, "You look good wit' your shirt off."

He smirked, looked down at his stomach and rubbed his abs. "I was in my room doin' a few crunches and pull-ups, somethin' small. Tryin' to keep my body tight."

I put my hand on my hip and in a sexy tone I said, "Pull-ups, huh?"

"Yeah, I got a pull-up bar in my room. Come on, let's go to my room and chill for a second." He nodded for me to follow him.

His room looked like a studio. There was beat-making equipment hooked up to his computer on the far side of the room. A huge keyboard sat on a rack next to the computer. Two huge speakers sat on the floor beside the wooden desk the computer sat on. His twin bed was against the wall, made up nice and neat. He had countless CDs. Right by his closet door was a pull-up bar. Boxes of Nikes, Timberlands, and New Balance were lined up against the wall.

I looked around and nodded. "Nice. I like."

He laughed and pointed behind me.

I turned around and saw the bookshelf that I missed. It was packed with books about making music, running businesses, and black history. And he had about four or five novels. I smiled and said, "I see you like to read."

"Yeah, but more importantly, I like to be informed. I gotta know what's goin' on wit' shit that I'm into. Feel me?"

"I like that."

He motioned toward his bed and said, "Have a seat, sexy."

I smiled and said, "Look at you. I just got here and you tryin' to get me in the bed already."

We both laughed.

"Go 'head wit' that shit. I was just tryin' to help you get comfortable."

I sat on his bed and set my Gucci bag beside me. I saw a picture of a dark-skinned dude on mirror above his dresser. The dude was locked up somewhere. "Who is that?" I said, pointing at the picture.

Face sat in an office chair in front of his computer. He spun around to face me. "That's my brother Greg."

"Where he at?" I asked, picking up a *Don Diva* magazine off the nightstand and flipping through it.

"He in the feds out Colorado, in a super-max joint." He said that like he was bitter about his brother's situation.

"I'm hip to that joint. That's where they got Wayne Perry. I got a cousin out there name Mustafa." On the real, I wanted to chill, so I didn't want to ask too many questions about his brother and risk upsetting him. Instead, I changed the subject to something I knew he loved: his music. "I see you got your own little studio up in here."

"Yeah, you can say that. I spend most of my time up in here, either makin' beats or working out," he smiled.

I moved closer to him, close enough to kiss his sexy lips. I reached out and softly rubbed the tattoo on his chest. "I can tell you work out. You fooled me, though. I thought you was just a skinny nigga, but wit' your shirt off, I see you nice. You workin' wit' a little somethin'."

He smiled. "Is that right? Let me find out you tryin' to stroke my ego."

"For real. I ain't tryin' to stroke you. I mean it, on everything. You look good. Nice chest, nice abs and all that. Believe what I'm sayin'."

He nodded. "I feel you." He looked me in the eyes and then looked down at my breasts. I had on a tight, short-sleeve Polo shirt that put my breasts on display. He looked at my thighs and placed his hand on

44

my leg, giving it a slight rub. I had on skin-tight jeans. He said, "You lookin' good your damn self, Niya. But that ain't nothing new; you always lookin' good."

I smiled and changed the subject. Nodding toward the studio equipment, I said, "Let me hear some of your work."
"Stop playin'. You for real?"

"I'm for real, boy. Let me see how good you are."

Face hit a few buttons, turned a few knobs, and just like that, a serious-ass beat came through the speakers and filled the room at low volume. It sounded like something Rick Ross would turn into a hit. Face said, "I don't want to turn it up too loud, my mother gotta get some rest."

"I feel you," I said, nodding my head. "I like that beat; it sounds good. You got a lot of talent. I'm impressed, Face."

"Thanks." He let me hear a few more beats. East Coast joints, down South joints, even a few R&B joints. They were all tight as shit.

"Damn, you do R&B joints too?"

"I do it all, Niya. I'm tryin' to eat. I gotta make this shit work. I want to be able to take care of my family wit' this shit here, feel me?"

I nodded in agreement. "Hell yeah, I feel you. If it don't make dollars, it don't make sense. Just stick wit' it. You gon' get on. Look how long it took people like Jay-Z to get on. They ain't do that shit overnight."

"I'ma ride it out. I don't ever give up." He cut the music off. "My brother be on me all the time about stickin' wit my music shit. He got a few connects he met in prison that's supposed to help me. I'm waitin' to see what's up with that right now. I'm sure in due time it will all come together."

I rubbed his shoulder and changed the subject again. "I ain't tell you I lost my job."

"Damn, for real?"

He sounded concerned. I respected that. He knew I was struggling on my own, trying my best to survive.

"Yeah, they had to let two people go, and I was one 'em. It's all good, though. That's how shit goes. I'll be okay. I'm always okay in the end."

"I got a few extra dollars. I sold a beat to them One Way dudes yesterday. If you need some money, I got you."

He melted my heart with that one. "Awww, thank you, Face, but I'm okay right now. That means the world to me, though."

"I fucks wit' you, Niya. If I had the world to myself, I'd give it all to you."

I couldn't stop blushing. "You layin' it on real thick, ain't you?"

He shrugged. "I'm feelin' you. What can I say? You my type, baby."

"Is that right?"

"Hell yeah, on everything. I mean that. I want to make you mine, Niya."

"I'm sure we can work somethin' out, boo," I said, then winked. I was flattered like shit. If he was to crack for the pussy at the moment, I'm sure the headboard on his bed would have been banging like a muthafucka, waking his mother up. "As far as you makin' me yours, I don't see that bein' too hard. I ain't been fuckin' wit' nobody lately. I can see me and you takin' things to another level. Let's see where things go."

Face smiled. "That sounds good to me." He kissed me on my lips, soft and quick.

"Okay, I didn't see that comin'."

"Time waits for no man, feel me? I had to take my chances."

I laughed, leaned over and tongue-kissed him. Showed him what a real kiss was. A passionate kiss. I ran my hands through his dreads as I kissed him. The smell of African Musk came from his hair. That turned me on even more than the way he was rubbing my back as we kissed. After parting lips with him, I took a deep breath. My nipples were hard, and my pussy was wet and throbbing. I wanted him inside me. He had aroused me, and I felt like rewarding him for such good work. From the look of the bulge between his legs, I could tell he wanted to get inside my pussy just as much as I wanted him to. He wanted me bad; it was written all over his face.

"We better stop before we start somethin' that's gon' have your mother wonderin' what's goin' on in here."

We both laughed.

"We can always go to your spot."

"Sounds good to me, but not tonight. Maybe another night, boo." I wasn't trying to dick tease, but after I thought about it, I just wasn't ready to give him the pussy yet. Soon. But not just yet.

He took it in stride and said, "I respect that. It's all good, sexy. You worth the chase and the wait."

I smiled. *He still trying to get in the pussy*, I thought.

Without another word about sex, he changed the subject. "So what you gon' do about work? You gon' start lookin' for another job?"

<u>New York Bound</u>

The alarm on the Range Rover went off around 1:15 a.m. I jumped out of the bed and ran outside in my Victoria's Secret sweat suit. I couldn't believe my eyes! Tish was fucking the Range up with a bat. She had smashed the headlights out. Busted the windows out. Fucked up the body of the truck. That was *my* Range. I was pissed the fuck off. Enraged! *This bitch must be crazy*, I thought. *She got to be out of her fucking mind.*

I rushed her, screaming, "Bitch, what the fuck is you doin' wit' your stupid ass?!"

She stopped and glared at me like a rabid dog ready to attack. "You dirty little bitch! Your slut-ass sister ain't been dead fifteen minutes and you already fuckin' Jay!"

"Bitch, I'ma beat your muthafuckin' ass!"

"Come on, ho!" She swung the bat and almost took my fucking head off.

I ducked. "Shit!" I came to my senses real quick. The bitch had a bat. Backing away, I screamed, "Put the bat down, bitch! I'll beat your muthafuckin' ass out here!"

"Don't run, bitch!" She chased me around the truck, swinging the bat. I refused to let her hit me with that bat.

The alarm on the Range continued to blare out of control, drawing attention. People started coming outside. Jay's 350 ZX bent the corner out of the blue. He slammed on the brakes, making the tires scream. Troy jumped out. "Ay, Tish, what the fuck you doin'?!" he shouted as he grabbed her and snatched the bat out of her hands. "Fuck is wrong wit' you?!"

Tish screamed, "Get the fuck off me, Troy!" She tried to snatch away from him, but he wouldn't let her go. "Let me go, Troy!"

I pulled the keys to the Range out and killed the alarm as a crowd began to form. Police sirens hit the air. The 4th District police station was right around the corner. Wasting no time, I turned my attention back to Tish, with fire in my eyes. "What's up now, bitch?" I said, walking toward her. "You ain't got the bat no more." I knew I'd tear her a new asshole, easy.

She screamed, "Fuck you, bitch!" Once again, she tried to snatch away from Troy, but his grip was too strong.

I went at her ass, but Troy snatched her out of my reach as I swung at her head with everything I had. He pushed me back, not aggressively, but just enough to keep me from punching her in the face while he was holding her.

Troy said, "Chill out, Niya."

Tish was calling me every bitch in the book.

I shouted, "Chill out?! Fuck that! You see what that bitch did to the truck?! Are you crazy?!"

"You lucky you wasn't in that truck, bitch! I know you fuckin' Jay, wit' your little dirty ass!"

Troy gave me a funny look. He then looked at Tish and said, "Come on, Tish, let me get you outta here before you get yourself locked up." Pulling her to the car, he looked at me and said, "Ay, Niya, go in the house before the police get here. I'll tell Jay what happened."

I looked at Tish, who was crying at this point, and said, "I'ma fuck you up soon as I catch you, bitch. Believe that."

As Troy stuffed her in the car, Tish yelled, "You ain't shit, bitch! Jay don't fuck wit' you for real. He just usin' your dumb—" Troy slammed the door, cutting her off. He jumped behind the wheel and pulled off.

I was steaming mad. I looked at the Range and shook my fucking head. That's all could do. Everybody was looking at me like I was crazy. I didn't even care. All I wanted was to get my hands on Tish; I was going to put my foot in her ass the very first chance I got. On everything I love.

I went back inside my building as the first police cars pulled up. Once inside, I called Jay and told him what went down.

He sighed. "I'll deal wit' Tish, don't even trip." He sounded frustrated.

"I'ma fuck that bitch up, Jay. You should see what the fuck she did to the truck. I can't believe that crazy bitch."

"Don't trip, I'll get the truck fixed. I'll deal wit' Tish, Niya."

"That's all good, but I'ma still put hands on that ho for talkin' all that shit about I'm fuckin' you and Jaz only been dead fifteen minutes. I ain't goin' for none of that shit she was talkin'. Fuck that! I'm hip to that bitch, for real. She can't even fight." I was heated, and it was clear in my tone of voice.

"Niya," Jay said calmly.

"What?!" I snapped.

"You gon' get your chance to fuck Tish up. I want you to beat her ass, baby girl, but you gotta chill out for now. I need you focused so you can make that trip up New York for me tomorrow. Don't worry about the truck. I'll take care of that. You'll be pushin' it like it's new in a few days. Okay?"

"Okay." I said. Something about the way he spoke to me calmed me like a sedative. His confidence and the way he always seemed to have shit under control made me listen when he spoke.

"Good girl," he said. "Now get some rest, Niya."

I got off the phone and went to bed.

* * *

Around 1:00 p.m. the next day, I was riding shotgun in Jay's royal-blue Bentley GT. 50 Cent was in the system. He was rapping that big-money shit. I was rockin' a pair of Prada shades, a blue Howard University T-shirt, Prada jeans and tennis shoes. I was carrying a blue Polo backpack. I was a little nervous, but my game face was on. I could deal with the situation. Hop on the train to New York, pick the shit up, hop on the train back to D.C., make a quick $2,000. How hard could it be? I could do it with ease.

Jay turned the music down, cut his eyes at me, and said, "You want somethin' to eat, Niya?"

I shook my head and said, "I'm good."

"You still thinkin' 'bout Tish, ain't you?"

"Fuck that bitch. I'ma put my foot in her ass first chance I get. You need to control your hoes," I said, rolling my eyes.

He smiled. "My hoes, huh?"

"Yeah, your hoes. You know you fuckin' her. Don't even fake like you not. I ain't slow. Don't no bitch act like that if she ain't fuckin' a nigga." I rolled my eyes again. "But that ain't my business. She just need to stay the fuck out my way, for real-for real."

Jay laughed as his cell phone went off with a Lil Wayne ringtone. He answered the phone and had a quick conversation. He was a smart street nigga. He never said more than he needed to on the phone. He then looked at me as we pulled up outside of Union Station in downtown D.C.

"Tish don't mean nothing to me, Niya," he coldly. "Look here, though, when you get to the spot, just ask for Twin. Get the shit and get right back on the train; don't make no extra stops."

I rolled my eyes, sucked my teeth, and said, "Come on, Jay, you know I ain't dumb."

He smiled, rubbed my thigh, and said, "I know you ain't dumb, Niya. I just wanted to remind you about the game plan. This shit is serious business here."

"I got you, Jay."

"Call me soon as you get up top, cool?"

"Got you."

"Good girl."

I shook my head and smiled as I stepped out of the car into the afternoon heat. There was a crowd of people moving about in a rush all around Union Station. I worked my way through the crowd and into the eatery. My mind was racing, but I was focused.

Thirty minutes later, I was on the train, headed North, listening to Lil Wayne on my iPod and reading a novel called *Angel*. I was sitting alone by the window. For some reason, I kept thinking about Face, wondering what he was doing. More than likely he was working on his music. He definitely had my attention. I wanted to spend more time with him, learn more about him. I hadn't been with a dude in a while, and it was time for a girl to get her issue.

My last boyfriend, Redds, was on all bullshit. He was 24 when I met him. I was 17. At first, he treated me real good, but once he knew I was feeling him, he started acting real cocky. I don't know what happened. Bitches used to call his phone all damn day. Every time I checked his phone there was a text message from a different bitch talking about getting with him. The shit was crazy, but I tried to overlook the shit because he always made sure I was okay. He spent so much time with me, taking me out to eat, taking me shopping — dropping paper like them old-school niggaz in the drug game. But in the end, I had to put my foot down and cut his dumb ass off. The last straw was when I found out he was fucking a close friend of mine named Jessica. I busted the windows of his Lexus and beat the shit out of Jessica as soon as I saw her ass. Fuck it, you live and you learn. Redds wanted to fuck me up for what I did to his car, but Jay told him he better lay back on any of those thoughts. Redds knew that if he put a finger on me, bullets would fly. Needless to say, Redds went on about his business and left me the fuck alone.

I wasn't feeling niggaz too tough after the shit with Redds. I had a few friends here and there after that—a bitch had needs—but nothing serious. But Face seemed different. He had me diggin' him.

The train ride to New York was nice and smooth, no sign of the law. I called Jay as soon as I got off the train at Penn Station. "I'm at Penn Station."

"Good girl. Catch a cab to the spot and ask for Twin. Simple as that, baby girl."

"I got you," I said, looking at the crowds of people were rushing around. Everything was moving so much faster than back home.

"See you when you get back, Niya."

"See you then." I ended the call and followed a crowd of people up the escalator. I was on my way.

I caught a cab to Harlem, taking in all the sights, and got out in front of an apartment building on St. Nichols Avenue. A few dudes in front of the building were looking at me like I was fresh meat. I hated that and, it showed on my face. I told the cab driver to wait for me, and I walked toward the building.

A cute brown-skin dude with cornrows said, "What's good, ma?" His New York accent was cute.

Playing no games and wasting no time, I killed the dude's aspirations and said, "I'm lookin' for Twin."

A tall dark-skin dude closest to the door said, "Follow me, ma."

I felt a little nervous, but I looked around and followed main man inside the building. I held the backpack tightly. We got on the elevator and went up to the fourteenth floor. We got the elevator and headed for the apartment at the end of the hallway. My Harlem escort knocked on the door. A few seconds later, locks were undone and a light-skin dude with curly hair opened the door. He looked like he was mixed, probably black and Spanish. Light-skin looked from the dark-skin dude to me and said, "D.C.?"

I wasn't ready for that, but I went with the flow. "Yeah. Twin?"

He opened the door wider and said, "Come in. Jay just called me a second ago. I'm Twin."

I stepped inside and looked around, feeling out of place. Something made me feel very uneasy.

Twin turned his attention to his man and said, "Black, I'm good, son."

Black nodded and headed back down the hallway.

Now it was just me and Twin—or so it seemed.

Twin shut the door and turned to me. "You're perfect."

Perfect?

"Huh?" I was confused.

"You look like a college student. Jake would never think you was breakin' the law, ma."

"Jake?" I frowned, not knowing who the hell jake was.

"The police."

I smiled. "Oh." I wanted to keep it moving, wasn't really with all the rappin' and small talk. "So what's up? You got somethin' for Jay?"

Twin smiled. "I like you, shorty." He looked to his left and said, "Goldie, bring that shoppin' bag in here for me, ma."

A brown-skin female came out of the back room wearing boy shorts and a white tank top. She was carrying a brown shopping bag. The look on her face made it clear that she was surprised to see me. I couldn't understand why the bitch was looking at me like that. She handed Twin the shopping bag and disappeared into the back room without a word. The way she looked at me had me feeling funny. I didn't know what was up with that.

Twin handed me the shopping bag and said, "It's all inside."

"Cool." I looked inside and saw three tightly wrapped bricks. "Let me put these joints in my backpack."

"Be my guest, ma." He waved toward the sofa.

I took a seat on the sofa and put the bricks in my backpack. "Catch you later, Twin," I said as I got up.

Looking me up and down, he said, "I hope so."

I gave him a half-ass smile.

He said, "You gon' leave without givin' me your name?"

I looked at him for second and didn't say a word. I didn't know the nigga from Adam. He wasn't a friend of mine, and for all I knew he was nothing more than a coke connect for Jay—a business partner. I said, "Jay ain't tell you my name?"

"He didn't get a chance to, just said his peoples was gon' be rockin' a Howard University T-shirt."

I smiled. "That's all he wanted you to know then."

Twin smiled with an approving nod. "You are one of a kind, D.C. That's what I'ma call you."

"Works for me, baby boy."

He opened the door to let me out. "Be safe, D.C."

"You too, Twin." I stepped into the hallway and saw the dude Black standing by the elevator. I headed his way, nervous as hell about the cocaine in my backpack.

I got on the elevator with Black and headed downstairs without speaking a word to him.

As soon as I stepped outside of the building a police car was just pulling up. *Fuck!* I couldn't believe my luck. NYPD was on the scene. My heart skipped a beat. Everything inside of me told me to turn around and run back inside the building. Four police jumped out and told all the dudes in front of the building to get against the wall. Black played it real smooth and kept walking like he wasn't even with me. The police didn't pay Black any attention, and he headed up St. Nicholas Avenue. My cab was still waiting. I put my game face on and walked to the cab as the cops searched the dudes on the wall. I swear to God, it seemed like the longest few seconds of my life. I was carrying prison time in my backpack, and it was all I could think about.

I made it to the cab and told the driver to get me back to Penn Station as fast as possible. I was trying to get the fuck out of New York. My heart was racing a mile a minute. My palms were sweaty. I couldn't stop thinking about the twenty-two years my moms was doing in the feds. I wondered if Young Jeezy had all this in mind when he recorded *Thug Motivation 101.*

* * *

When I got back to D.C., Jay was waiting for me outside of Union Station in his 350 ZX. I didn't feel safe until I was inside the car headed up 7th Street. I wasn't sure if I could make another trip like that for him. My freedom needed to be put before everything else.

Jay smiled at me and said, "You did good, baby girl." He patted me on my thigh.

I acted like it was nothing and shrugged. I'd never tell him I was second-guessing the whole trip. I'd never tell him I was scared to death when I stepped out of that building and saw NYPD in action. Nah, I'd never tell Jay any of that. I needed him to have confidence in me; I needed him to feel as though he could count on me at all times.

Jay said, "Twin said you handled yourself well. But I been knew you was a rider. That ain't nothin' new to me. Feel me?"

"It's an uptown thing; you know how that go."

He laughed. "Yeah, I feel you." He kept his eyes in his rearview mirror, always on point, as we headed up Georgia Avenue.

I handed the backpack to Jay. For some reason, I wanted it as far away from me as possible.

Jay cut his eyes at me and said, "So what you think about the trip? You think you can handle somethin' like that for me here and there? I need somebody I can trust to take care of that."

The thought of $2,000 for a few hours of work seemed real appealing. I couldn't see it being a long-term thing, but I could use the money at the time. I said, "Yeah, I think I could handle that for you."

He smiled.

Jay handed me $2,000 in big bills when we walked into my apartment. It was all the money I had to my name, and I had to live off of it until I got another job or made another move to come up on some change. On the real, after making the trip to New York, I wasn't even interested in getting another job. I felt I could make ends meet by other means. At least for the meantime.

Sitting on the sofa rolling up some weed, Jay said, "Ay, Niya, I need you to cook that coke up for me when you get a chance. Cool?"

I smirked and said, "Boy, let me find out you movin' all that work in the streets and you don't know how to whip coke yet," I said as I ate a bag of potato chips.

"Never took the time out to learn. Fuck it."

I shook my head. "Don't worry, I got you." I grabbed the remote and turned the TV from ESPN to "106 and Park." "I'll take care of that after I order somethin' to eat. Cool?"

"Yeah, no problem. Take your time. Just do it for me as soon as you can. I have a few dudes to hit across town."

Jay finished rolling the Backwood and set it on the coffee table beside a *F.E.D.S.* magazine he was reading. He removed his Glock .40 from his waistband and set it on the table as well, making himself at home. He stood up, dug into his pocket, and pulled out a lighter that looked like a small pistol. He tossed me the lighter and said, "Put it in the air. I gotta go to the bathroom real quick."

I fired the weed up as Jay went to take care of his business in the bathroom. I could tell the weed was that good shit after first hit. Shit, I started feeling nice and kicked my feet up on the coffee table. The $2,000 in my pocket would take care of rent, food, money for my moms, and a little extra for whatever I wanted. I was good for a second.

Jay came back from the bathroom and went straight to the kitchen. He got a tall glass of ice water and made his way back to the sofa. I passed him the Backwood. He took a few hits and passed it back to me. He then pulled out some E pills and popped one, downing it with water. "Want one?"

I shook my head. "Nah, I'm good, thanks."

He put the pills back in his pocket. Moments later, his cell phone went off. He answered it and had a quick conversation about business, although he didn't really say much about business at all. When he got off the phone, he got up and said, "I gotta roll. You gon' have that shit cooked up for me later, right?"

I blew smoke in the air and shook my head. "Yeah, give me 'bout an hour or so."

"Good girl," he said as he grabbed his pistol and left.

I smoked the rest of the weed to the head and decided to cook the bricks for Jay before I ordered my food. I wondered how many trips to New York I would be making. Once a week would be $8,000 a month. I could make some things happen with that kind of paper.

I couldn't let my moms find out, though. She would be highly fucked up about me fucking with drugs. Nevertheless, I had to survive. I was on my own.

<u>Dollars Make Sense</u>

"You fuckin' wit" Jay now?" Lisa asked me as we sat in my living room the following afternoon.

I hated people in my business, but Lisa was my girl, so I let her slide.

"Me and Jay cool. He be lookin' out for me," I said as I painted my toenails. He know my situation fucked up right now—no job, on my own and shit. Out of respect for my mother and Jaz, he just be makin' sure I'm okay, feel me?"
Lisa gave me a funny look and smiled. "If you say so, boo. I mean ... he let you push the Range and everything. That's what a nigga do for wifey, you know what I mean?"

She was starting to pick too much, and it was getting on my fucking nerves.

"Lisa, you readin' too much into shit. It ain't like that," I said it as nicely as I could. But the look on my face and my tone of voice screamed: Leave it alone! Stop asking so many fucking questions!

She caught on and changed the subject. "So what's up wit' the bitch Tish? You tryin' to go see her ass today?"

"Yeah, that bitch need some act right," I said with attitude for days.

Lisa couldn't stand Tish either. Tish had fucked her boyfriend when they went to Cardozo High School together. Lisa beat the shit out of Tish over that one there. Tish had a history of shit like that.

I planned to put my foot in Tish's ass as soon as I caught up with her. I was going to make the shit Lisa did to her look like a day at the salon. On everything.

My cell phone rang. "Pass me that phone, Lisa." The caller came up as unavailable. I knew it was my moms calling. I answered the phone and pressed 5 without listening to the recording. "What's up, Ma?"

"I'm holdin' on, Niya," whe said with a lot of prison noise in the background. Her voice seemed upbeat. That was a blessing. I hated to hear her stressed out in there.

"Did you get the books I sent you?" I asked as I let me toenails dry.

"I got them. Thanks, baby."

"I'ma send you some money later on today when I go out."

"What would I do without you, Niya?"

I smiled. "Let's not even talk about that. Don't wanna' talk that up."

"Yeah, you right. So how's work?"

Moms had enough to worry about. I didn't want to tell her about the trip to New York. I hated lying to my moms, but I had to at the time. "Everything is cool at work. I plan to come see you before the month is out," I said, trying to change the subject. "Jay be lettin' me use his truck."

"What's up with you and Jay, Niya?"

That came outta left field. "Huh? What you mean by that?"

"You and Jay real close, ain't you? I understand he be lookin' out for you since Jaz's death, but he lettin' you hold his car and truck ... what's up with that, Niya? Ain't nothin' in this world free. You know what I mean, baby?"

I was quiet for a second. My moms was far from slow. "Ma, ain't nothin' up wit' me and Jay. He like a brother to me, that's all."

"Niya, don't fool yourself. He ain't your brother; he's a man, and you are a young woman. That's how it is. You understand where I'm coming from?"

I nodded. "Yeah, I understand, Ma."

"Now, I ain't gon' insinuate nothin', but I'ma tell you like I kept tellin' Jasmine: I don't want you hooked up with no street dudes. Dudes in the life only bring trouble, one way or another. You hear me?"

"Yeah, I hear you."

"What's up other than that, Niya? I ain't gon' call you and get on you. You're grown now."

"I'm cool. Just sittin' here wit' Lisa doin' my toes." I couldn't stop thinking about what she'd just said to me. "Oh yeah—I knew it was somethin' I wanted to ask you."

"What?"

"I was readin' this article in the paper about this dude that had 30 years in prison, right, but he appealed his case and got out of prison. What's up wit' your case? Don't you have an appeal in?"

Moms laughed. "Baby, I been filing everything I can to the courts to get out of here. It's a long battle. Right now it seems like ain't nothing working," she sighed, frustrated.

"What if we got you some big-shot lawyer? Would that help?"

"First of all, lawyers are full of shit. They tell you anything to get your money, then they tell you some other shit once you pay 'em. Second of all, we don't have no big-shot lawyer money, Niya. I'm good with the lawyer I have right now. If I could just cut my time down some, I'd be happy. Anyway, I have some stuff in court right now. I'm waiting to see what the judge says."

"I understand, Ma. I was just wondering." I still felt that if I could get her a better lawyer it would help her get out of prison faster.

"Look, baby, this phone is about to hang up on us. I love you. Talk to you later."

"Love you too. I'ma send you that money today. Send me another list of books you want too."

"I will. I'll—"
The phone hung up. I shut my cell phone and set it beside me.

"How's your mother doin'?" Lisa asked.

"She's okay, holdin' on," I said. I was thinking about looking into a lawyer for her. Money always makes a difference in the court system.

"I don't know how she does it in there, Niya. If I had all that time to do, I'd go crazy, for real." She then pulled an E pill out of her pocket and popped it with a sip of water.

"Moms is a soldier, Lisa. She gon' be alright, no matter what."

"I feel you." She pulled another pill out of her pocket. "Want one?"

"I'm good." I stood up, careful not to mess up my toes. "I need to send my moms some money. Can you take me to the post office?"

"Yeah, that ain't nothin'. I got you."

* * *

I jumped in Lisa's Escalade and we were on our way to the post office. I couldn't believe she was making so much money stripping. Her Escalade was tight as shit. The system was top-of-the-line. She had T.I.'s What You Know pumpin' through the powerful speakers. T.I. was my baby. When we pulled up at the light on 14th Street all eyes were on us. Her truck always grabbed attention, it had two seven-inch TV monitors in the headrests, one in the visor. She even had a fifteen-inch TV that dropped from the ceiling with a DVD player. The truck was sitting on twenty-fours.

The light turned green and we began cruising up 14th Street. It was nice outside, everybody and their mother was outside. I loved my city.

I looked at Lisa and said, "You got enough TVs up in this joint, don't you?"

She laughed. "I like to do it big ... it ain't trickin' if you got it, feel me?"

I died laughing, Lisa was funny as shit.

She said, "So what you gon' do now you don't got the job at the book store no more?"

I shrugged. I really wasn't trying to think about that. "I'll make a few moves. I'ma eat, believe that."

"I know that's right, bitch. A bitch gotta eat out here." Lisa slid on her Prada shades. "Shit, you might as well come get some of this stripper money I'm gettin'. You got the body for it, girl. You damn sure got the looks. And you can dance. The shit is sweet, Niya. I'm tellin' you some good shit.

I laughed. "Nah, I'm good. I'ma leave that to you, Lisa. That's too much for me."

"Too much for you?!" Lisa said with a confused look on her face. "You better stop trippin', Niya. Ain't shit to it. Show a little skin, shake your ass for a second, and collect your paper. I made damn near a $1,000 last night alone. Easy paper."

"Shit, $1,000?" I asked, raising my eyebrows. My girl Tender was only making something like $1,500 a week when she was stripping. "That's a nice piece of change right there."

"I'm killin' 'em, Niya. I ain't gon' lie to you. The shit is sweet; it's like takin' candy from a baby."

I gave what she was saying some serious thought for a second, but my cell phone went off before I could say a word. It was Jay. I told Lisa to hold fast for a second and took the call. "What's up?"

"Ay, Niya, I need you," Jay said. Gunfire was going off in the background—a lot of it. It sounded like a shootout with automatic weapons.

"Where the hell you at? What's goin' on?" I said, concerned. My heart was racing like a speeding Ducati. Lisa was all in my mouth, sucking up every word.

Jay said, "I'm good, baby girl. I'm at the gun range."

I calmed down when he said that.

He continued. "Ay, you know that last pair of tennis shoes you got? The ones you bought when you went shoppin' up New York?"

"Yeah, I'm wit' you." I caught on quick.

"My man fucked up. He play ball for Howard, right, and he need a fresh pair of basketball shoes before the game start. I'm all the way out Maryland, and I can't get back to the city in time for the game. Can you meet 'em around the way and give 'em the shoes for me?"

"Yeah, I got you. It ain't nothin'," I said.

"Good girl. You the best, Niya. I got you when I see you. My man gon' call you in 'bout twenty minutes, so be ready."

"I got you."

Lisa wasted no time asking questions. "What's up, Niya? Everything okay?"

"Yeah, everything cool. I just need to take care of something real quick." Lisa knew that meant I wasn't trying to talk about the situation. Simple as that.

We returned to the conversation about how lucrative stripping was. We hit the post office, and I sent my moms $250. We hit the weed spot and headed back around the way. I needed to duck Lisa for a second so I could handle the situation for Jay. I told her I'd catch her a little later because I had to change clothes and catch a cab downtown to look into a lawyer for my moms' case.

Lisa went for it and decided to go holla at her man around the corner.

I ran inside my apartment and got the last brick of hard white I'd cooked up for Jay and put it in an old Gucci shopping bag I had in my closet. My cell phone went off a few seconds later. It was a dude named Dice. He said that Jay told him to holla at me. He said he was outside in a gray Crown Vic. I told him I'd be out in a second.

I grabbed the shopping bag and stepped outside. I spotted the Crown Vic and walked over to the driver's window. Dice rolled down the window, and I handed him the shopping bag. No one seemed to be paying me any attention, but I was still nervous.

Dice looked inside the shopping bag and said, "Tell Jay I said it's all good."

"Cool." I was ready to get the hell out of the heat. As I turned to walk away, Dice called me.

"Ay, ain't you forgettin' somethin', sexy?" He held up a brown paper bag.

Jay didn't tell me anything about getting something in return for the coke. All he said was for me to give the coke to Dice.

Dice said, "You gon' take the money or what, sexy?"

I grabbed the paper bag. The stacks of money inside were heavy. I said, "Good lookin'." I stepped off with the money.

Dice pulled off.

I heard a door open behind me as I walked down the hallway inside my building.

A voice called out, "Niya!"

I turned around and saw a big-ass brown-skin dude—Suge Knight big. He had a baby face, though. I couldn't believe my eyes. It was my little homie, Bam. He was a year younger than I was and lived on the same floor as me. His mother was on coke, so me and Jaz used to look out for him from time to time over the years. However, last year he got locked up for carrying a pistol and was sent to some juvenile lock-up joint in Maryland to serve time. I don't know what they were feeding him when he was locked up, but he'd grown about three or four inches and put on a lot of weight. He wasn't fat, just big as shit.

"What, you don't remember me no more, Niya?" Bam said as he walked towards me. He smiled. His voice was all deep now. He had dreads down to his shoulders.

I smiled, looking up at his huge ass. "Damn, boy, you got big as shit."

He laughed as he gave me a big hug. "I know. I was eatin' like shit down that joint. Eatin' and lifting weights."

"You need to be playing football somewhere, boy."

"I ain't got time for no football, Niya. I just got out. I'm trying to eat. I need some paper."

I looked Bam up and down. He still had on his institution clothes.
"You better take your time out here. Don't get caught up bullshittin'."
I had real love for Bam. He was like a little brother to me. I didn't want to see him go back to jail.

His face got real serious. "I heard about Jaz. That's fucked up. I was hurt about that shit. I'm sorry that shit went down like that."

It pained me to think about what happened to my sister. "Yeah, I'm still fucked up about that. I don't even like talkin' about it, for real."

"I feel you. My bad ... I ain't mean to make you sad."

"It's cool, Bam."

He rubbed the little bit of hair that was growing on his face and said, "I gotta roll. I got some things to do real quick." He gave me another hug.

"You be good and stay out of trouble, okay?"

He gave me a funny look and said, "I'll do my best." He then jogged down the hall, looking like a gaint.

I went inside my apartment and sat on the sofa. I took the rubber bands off of the stacks of money and counted the bread. It was $28,000 in twenties, fifties, and one hundreds. It was a lot of money. The most I'd ever seen at one time. Jay made $28,000 off one brick of coke that I cooked up for him. I wondered what he'd paid for the brick when it was in powder form. I mean, I wasn't green. I understood the coke game on the street level from growing up around Rittenhouse Street, but I didn't really know much about the weight game. However, I did know that it was more money in the drug game than it was in stripping.

I put the rubber bands back on the money and put it back in the paper bag. I had money on my mind.

Face called me a little while later. I was pleased to hear his voice. We spoke for a few minutes and made plans to get together later. I looked forward to spending some time with Face.

As soon as I got off the phone with Face, there was a knock at my door. I went to see who it was. It was Jay. I let him in.

"What's up, Niya?" Jay said, hugging me. I shut the door. "Everything went well wit' my man Dice?"

"Yeah, it was all good. Why you ain't tell me I was supposed to get the money from the dude?"

"I didn't want to say too much on the phone. I knew you would catch on. You smart, baby girl."

I blushed a little.

Jay pointed at the paper bag and said, "That's the money right there?" He grabbed the bag and looked inside.

"I counted it. It's twenty-eight thousand."

Jay smiled as he sat on the sofa. He peeled off some bills and sat them on the coffee table. "That's you right there, Niya." He nodded toward the money.

I picked the money up as I sat on the sofa. It was $1,000. Damn, I made $1,000 for handing Dice a brick of coke for Jay. Sweet!
"Jay, let me ask you somethin'."

"What's good?"

"The dude Twin that you sent me to see, how much he charge you for a brick of powder?"

Jay smiled as if he could read my mind. "Me and Twin got a special situation. He only charge me seventeen for them joints. He kinda like owe me a favor or two, but that's another story."

I nodded my head as I did the math. "So you pay seventeen and turn around and push them joints for twenty-eight, huh? That's a quick $11,000 right there."

"Shit, sometimes I sell them joints for thirty or thirty-two thousand, depending on who it is. I also break them joints down and sell 62s and ounces, shit like that. It's all about the flip and what I got to work with. Why you asking me all these questions? You act like you want in or something."

"Dollars make sense. I just wanted to know how it works on that level, feel me?"

Jay nodded.

"You said the situation you got wit' Twin is special. What you mean by special?" I was wondering if I could buy a brick of powder if I had $17,000."

"I saved Twin's life when we was in the feds at this joint in Lee County. Niggaz was 'bout to put that knife in his ass over some bullshit, but me and my man Rome stepped on the scene and stopped the shit. Twin was grateful. He told me whenever I got out he was gon' make sure he did somethin' nice wit' me. He was a man of his word." Jay winked.

"Oh, I understand."

"You thinkin' 'bout gettin' your feet wet?" He had a smirk on his face.

I shook my head. "I wouldn't say that just yet. I just wanted to know what was up. If shit is that sweet, I don't see why I couldn't snatch a piece of that money, you know?"

With a serious look on his face, Jay said, "It's a dirty game, Niya. You gotta really know what you doin'. Anybody can be the feds. Muthafuckas gon' want what you got, and they gon' be willin' to kill you for it. You gon' have to second-guess your friends and some more shit. I'm tellin' you, it's a dirty game, baby girl. Trust me."

I thought about what he was saying for a second. It was a price to pay for everything in life. My moms always said that. Risks were a part of life. This I knew. I took a huge risk making the trip to New York for Jay, on the real, but I did it.

Changing the subject, Jay said, "The Range will be ready tomorrow, so you'll be back in action in no time, baby girl."

I smiled. "I'ma still put my foot in Tish's ass. Soon as I catch her."

Jay shook his head and laughed.

I Need Love

Face and I caught a cab to Georgetown and went to the movies. After that, we grabbed something to eat and caught a cab back to his spot. He paid for everything. He said he didn't want me to spend a dime on anything, even though I told him I had a few dollars. He said the man in him wouldn't allow him to let me spend my money when he was taking me out. I liked that, thought it was cute. He earned big points with me with that one. I must admit, we had a good time. It was good to get out and chill for a minute. I needed that. On top of that, his mother had gone to Baltimore to visit her sister, so we had the apartment to ourselves. We sat in the bedroom and smoked a little weed while watching *The Wire* on DVD.

Feeling nice, I said, "Them Baltimore niggaz be movin' that blow like that for real." I loved *The Wire*. I was feeling the way Marlow had shit locked on B-more's west side. He reminded me of Jay.

"Yeah, them B-more niggaz do be movin' that blow like shit. I got cousins out there. I used to stay with them when I was like 13, 14."

My phone went off. It was a text from Jay asking what I was doing later on. I hit him back real quick and told him I was chillin' with Face. He hit right back and told me to call him as soon as I could.

"Is everything cool?" Face asked.

"Yeah, everything is cool. Jay must need me to do something for him, but I'm chillin' right now." I put my phone up and said, "So where your peoples from?"

"West side, same area they shot *The Wire* in. My cousins used to do their thing in Lexington Terrace." Face put his arm around me as he spoke. We were sitting at the foot of the bed. Changing the subject, he said, "You know what?"

"What?" I smiled, wondering if he could tell that my nipples were hard under my Stop Snitching T-shirt.

"I'm tryin' to talk about something else right now," he said with a sexy-ass look in his eyes—a look that made me wet between the legs.

I gave him a sexy look, licked my lips, and said, "What you tryin' to talk about then?"

Softly, he traced my left nipple with his finger. It sent chills through my body. "Your nipples hard as shit, Niya." He pinched my nipple. That made me wetter. I squirmed a little bit as I felt the wetness between my legs begin to build.

I wanted to give him the pussy, wanted to feel him inside me, stroking me deep and hard. I needed it. I wondered if he could handle this pussy. Shit, he worked out, was in good shape. But could he fuck was the question. High, horny, and wet, I needed to be fucked good. It wasn't a whole lot to it. That's exactly what I was looking for at the time. Anything less would be a waste of time. All kinds of thoughts raced through my mind when he pinched my nipple. Damn, I wanted to wrap my legs around him and throw the pussy on him.

Face kissed me. His tongue tasted like apple Jolly Ranchers. I closed my eyes and put my arms around him, pulling him closer to me. Our kiss was ongoing, heating up our bodies, getting us overly aroused. He squeezed my breast. It made me moan a little. I purred like a cat in heat.

He pulled my T-shirt over my head with ease and said, "I wanna' make you mine, Niya."

I smiled and helped him with my bra. He took my breasts in his strong, warm hands and squeezed them. I moaned, "You are doin' a good job at makin' me yours." I slid my hand inside his pants and felt his manhood growing thick.

He sucked my nipples, and it drove me crazy. My insides were on fire.

I moaned, "I want you inside me, Face." I began to undo his pants. "Take it out. Let me see it, Face." I unzipped his pants and pulled out his manhood. It was hard and still growing right between my fingers. Slowly, I stroked it. I licked my lips and looked from his erection to his eyes and then back to his erection. I wanted him, in my mouth, in my pussy. I didn't care, I just wanted him inside me.

He rubbed his hand through my hair as his erection grew to full strength. I was so wet I began to wonder if my juices had soaked through my panties and jeans and onto his sheets.

Stroking his erection I said, "Damn, boy, you are blessed."

He smiled, proud that I respected his size.

"You are so hard," I said, still stroking his dick.

He said, "Take your clothes off, Niya."

I began to undress. "Take yours off."

He smiled with lustful passion in his eyes.

Seconds later we were undressed, in his bed. I got on top of him, had my hands on his hard chest, and looked down into his blood-shot eyes like, Fuck me! I could feel his hardness between my legs, pressing up against my clit. I was coating his dick with my wetness.

I said, "You got condoms in here?"

He nodded. He reached over. opened the nightstand drawer, and pulled out a Magnum.

I snatched the condom out of his hand and tore it open. "Let me do this, boo."

Face smiled and squeezed my ass, sinking his fingers deep into my soft flesh. His touch alone felt good.

I grabbed his manhood and rolled the Magnum on it eagerly. If I didn't get him inside of me soon I was going to die. Raising up just a little bit, I used my hand to guide him inside of me. "Ahhh," I said. It felt so good. It had been a while since I had let a nigga get inside of me. I frowned a little as I eased down on his dick. He felt larger than he looked. I gasped. "Ahhh, shit," I moaned as my eyes rolled back in my head. The pleasure spread throughout my whole body. Slowly, I began to slide up and down on his manhood, riding him as if I couldn't get enough. My moans became nonstop as he filled my insides with every inch he had to offer.

He whispered, "You tight as shit, Niya. So ... damn ... tight, girl." He lifted his hips, pushing his manhood up inside me more and more with every stroke. My breasts began to bounce as I dug into his chest with my nails, leaving my mark on him. He grunted, "Ride this dick, Niya." I began to throw it on him harder.

"Shhhhhhhit," I moaned. I loved the way he was fucking me. I got aggressive and rode his dick harder, bouncing on it like it would be my last chance in life. I was creaming all over the place as he wrapped his hands around my waist and began to pull me down on his thrusting dick. "Ssssssss ... oh yeah, fuck me, fuck me, fuck me, fuck me good, Face." We were sweating hard, fucking intensely. The bed springs were crying, and the headboard was trying to beat a hole in the wall. It felt like he was in my stomach with every pounding stroke. I moaned, "You feel like ... oh shit ..." My eyes rolled back in my head. "I'm 'bout to cum. Oh my God, I'm 'bout to cum ... fuck me harder. Aahhhhhh, yeah ... fuck me, fuck me, fuck me ... don't—aaaaaaaahhhh!" I screamed as I exploded. I came so hard it made me feel light-headed.

Looking me in the eyes, grabbing my hips firmly, Face whispered, "Cum all over this dick. Keep cummin' for me, Niya."

I was in another world as my orgasm kicked in the front door. I was shaking. I closed my eyes, gritted my teeth, bit my bottom lip, and moaned like he was killing me. I didn't care if all of D.C. could hear me. I was loving the dick, loving the way he was fucking me. I didn't want it ever end.

"Damn, this pussy good, Niya," Face said, still pulling me down on his dick hard and fast, filling me with all that I could take.

"Ahhhhh, shit!" I shouted as I came a second time. I began to feel faint. I kept moving my hips, enjoying every minute of my orgasm. "I'm cummin' again ... Face, I'm cummin' again!" I shouted that countless times as I rode my orgasm like it was a powerful motorcycle. I was shaking uncontrollably, cummin' as hard as I had ever cum. "Oooooo, sssssss, shit."

Face fucked me harder as I came. He said, "I'm about to cum, Niya, I'm 'bout to bus'."

That turned me on, made me give him all I had left. I rode him hard and fast, wanting to make him cum. I wanted him to cum just as hard as he had made me cum. "You like that? You like bein' in this pussy?"

With his eyes closed, he grunted. I could feel him cumming, filling the condom. "I'm cumin'. Damn, I'm cummin'. I'm cumin inside you."

I liked the sound of that. Cumming inside of me, even with the rubber on, felt so damn good. As we slowed down I said, "You feel so good inside me." I was trying to catch my breath.

He said, "Damn, Niya, you did the muthafucka'."

I laughed a little. "You ain't do a bad job yourself. I love the way you fucked me. I'ma need some more of that," I said, still on top of him with his erection dying inside of me. I lay down on him, my breasts pressed against his chest.

"I been wantin' to get in that pussy for the longest." He rubbed my damp back and squeezed my ass.

"You wasn't tryin' hard enough," I joked. "But you got the pussy now, so you good?"

He laughed. "Yeah, I'm good for right now. I want to taste you, though. Let me eat that pussy."

He turned me on with that one. I smiled. My pussy was still tingling with his limp dick resting inside me. I said, "I'm game. What you waitin' for?" I shivered at the thought of him eating my pussy. Face was my kinda nigga.

He said, "I'ma make you cum wit' my tongue. I'ma make you cum so many times you gon' wanna move in."

"Yeah, right," I laughed as I got up, feeling his dick ease out of me. I positioned myself over his face and took a seat. In a sexy voice, I said, "Please tell me you know what you doin', boo."

He held my ass and said, "You gon' love me when it's all over."

Shit! His tongue ... oh, God! His tongue made me moan instantly. If he didn't hold me in place I would have jumped off of his face. He began to devour me, using his tongue and fingers in all the right places, as if he already knew what I liked. I felt trapped on top of his face. Trapped between pleasure and pain. His tongue game was off the meter. He licked circles around my clit. Breathed on it. Bit it, fanned his tongue across it as he held it between his teeth. Oh my God, I swear I was about to pass out, I bullshit you not. I begged, "Stop ... that's enough ... please, I can't take it no more ..." I was grinding my hips against his face, steady and slow. Dangerously close to cumming all over his face. "Face!" I shouted.

"You shouldn't have talked all that fly shit. 'Please tell me you know what you doin', boo,'" he said, mocking me.

I was losing control. I hated that. I couldn't focus. Face was in control now. His tongue was his weapon of conquest and I was conquered. "Ahhh ... I'm cummin'." My eyes rolled back in my head. I squeezed my breasts hard, bit my lip and moaned. I wanted to scream and shout, but instead I moaned from deep within, "Ooooooo ... God ... you got it ... you got it, Face ... you got it ... oh, God, you got it ..." It was too intense. My orgasm was just too damn intense. It made me fall off of his face and onto to my side. My head was spinning. Breathing hard, I looked at Face and said, "You win, baby, you win." I smiled.

With my juices on his face, Face said, "We can do this all night long—if you down." He smiled and winked at me.

Playfully, I gave him a scared looked and said, "I'm all yours. Don't hurt me."

* * *

Bright sunrays shone on my face, waking me up. I looked at the clock on the top of the computer. It was 11:38 a.m. I was under the covers and didn't want to move. I was lying next to Face, naked, his arms around me. Our bodies were pressed together. I could still feel the impression he left between my legs. A lustful smile spread across my face. We had the headboard banging against the wall until damn near 4 a.m. I came so many times I lost count. Face put in work. I give him that. We could definitely hook up again … and again and again. I was feeling him like shit.

I sat up and stretched. That must've awoken Face. He looked up at me, yawned, and said, "Damn, baby, I'm in love." He smiled.

I laughed. "Cut the jokes out, boy."

He laughed as swell. "I dreamnt about you."

I smiled and played along. "What did you dream about? And don't tell me you had no wet dream either."

"I dreamed about eatin' your sweet pussy."

My pussy tingled. "Dreams like that come true, but you already know that, don't you?"

"True, I can stamp that there." He smirked. "My dreams came true all night long."

I smiled. "Is that right, boo?"

"Make no mistake about it. I can't wait for my dreams to come true again."

"Well, maybe we can make them come true more often, but right now I need a shower. Bad." I said.

"Make yourself at home. My mother won't be back for a while. Everything you need's in the bathroom.

I got up and took a hot shower, thinking about Face the whole time. What if we had a relationship? What would it be like? A thousand thoughts went through my mind as I washed my body and let the hot water soothe me.

When I got out of the shower, I ran right into Face. He wanted to get in the shower with me but he waited too long. With a sad face, he got in the shower alone. I laughed. He was funny.

I got dressed in his bedroom. While I was waiting for him to get out of the shower, I checked my text messages. I was shocked to see that Troy had sent me a text wanting to know if he and I could hang out later. That was new. Sure, he tried to holla at me all the time in person, but he'd never texted that to my phone. I shook my head and smiled. Niggaz just don't quit when they want the pussy. I ran through my other messages and then called a cab.

Face drew my attention to him when he came in the room wearing nothing but a towel. His body looked so good. Just looking at him made me want to fuck him one more time before I left. But that would have to wait. I looked at him and said, "I hate to run on you, but I got a few things to take care of, so I called a cab. We gon' get together later. Cool?"

He made another sad face and said, "You breaking my heart already."

I laughed. "Boy, stop playin'. Cut it out. We can get together later. I promise."

"I'm gon' hold you to that too."

I smiled and gave him a kiss.

* * *

I stepped outside of the building to wait for my cab on 14th Street. It was already hot outside, and people were everywhere. A car horn blared and grabbed my attention. I was wearing the shit out of my True Religion jeans. knew that was the reason homeboy in the 745 was hitting the horn, trying to get my attention. I smiled and looked to my left when someone caught my eye. I was instantly pissed the fuck off, ready to attack. Tish was coming down the street in a tank top, booty shorts, and a pair of heels with straps around her ankles. Every car that passed her was blowing the horn at her ho ass. We locked eyes, and I knew it was on.

I frowned and hissed, "I got your ass now, bitch!" I rushed her. I punched her right in the mouth and made her stumble in her heels. She tried to grab my hair but I caught her with another quick blow to the side of her jaw and made her cry out in pain. She scratched my neck trying to grab me again, swinging wild punches that wasn't about shit. I ate her punches like ice cream. I was all over her ass with my blows, trying to take her head off. "Talk that fly shit now, bitch! Talk that shit now!"

People began to stare as I beat the shit out of her. I was making her look like a rag doll. She scratched my face, screaming, "Get off me, bitch! Get the fuck off me!"

"Shit!" I shouted. I felt her nails dig into my skin. "Bitch!" I slammed her head against the parked car and kneed her in the gut hard as shit. She grunted. I could tell that I knocked the wind out of her. My next blow bashed her in the eye and made her scream like she'd been hit with a weapon. I grabbed a handful of her hair and pulled her head down. I kneed her right in the face. It felt like I broke something. I kneed her about two or three more times and then slung her ho ass to the ground as if she was weightless.

She grabbed her bloody face, rolling over on the sidewalk like she was in serious pain. "Shit, my nose! Bitch, you broke my nose! You broke my fuckin' nose!"

"So what! You asked for it, bitch!" I kicked her in the stomach hard as shit. "Ho-ass, bitch!" I kicked her again. "You wanna beat up trucks and shit, huh?" I kicked her again, this time in the face. "Keep my sister's name out your muthafuckin' mouth, whore!"

Tish moaned and stopped moving. On everything, she wasn't moving at all, only moaning like a wounded animal.

I looked around and felt a little nervous when I saw a number of people standing around looking at me like I was crazy. I kicked Tish in the back one last time. "Dirty bitch!"

I came to my senses when I heard police sirens. I looked up and saw a police car coming down 14th Street. Without a second thought, I took off running down the block and hit the alley.

* * *

The next day it seemed like everybody was outside around my way. A crap game was in full swing right outside of my apartment. Jay and a few other dudes in his circle were on the scene. Bam and a few young homies were smoking, drinking, joanin', and looking for something to get in to. I was sitting in Lisa's Escalade talking to her and my girl Terri. Jay-Z was on the radio — WKYS, 93.9. I was telling them how I beat the shit out of Tish, and they were loving it, eating up every detail.

"I'm glad you put that bitch in her place," said Terri. She needed a serious ass kickin'. I don't know what she thought she was doin', comin' around here fuckin' up Jay's Range like that. She couldna thought she was gon' get away wit' no bullshit like that."

Terri was a year older than I was. We'd been friends since I was like 6. She was a cute light-skin girl with long, silky hair and a small, sexy frame. She was tall, about an inch under six-feet. Her stand-out feature was her cat eyes—they seemed to change from gray to hazel without warning. Terri was cool as shit, but she could be wild at times. When it was time, she was 'bout that drama.

Lisa said, "I heard some girls in the club last night talkin' 'bout how you put Tish in the hospital. You must've punished that ass for real."

"I broke her nose. That'll hold her."

Terri laughed. "I wish I was there. I would've paid to see you beat that ass. I know if I was there, I would've stomped her ass out."

We all laughed.

As we sat in the truck laughing and talking, I saw some confusion going on over where Bam and his little crew were. Bam was arguing with one of the older dudes who ran with Jay—a dude named Latif. Latif was about 26. He had to be about 200 pounds and stood about 5'10", yet he was still smaller than Bam's overgrown 17-year-old ass. The argument looked heated. They were getting loud, all up in each other's face. A small crowd was growing around them. I could tell that there was going to be trouble. Jay stepped up and tried to defuse the situation. Bam wasn't trying to hear whatever Jay was saying—I could tell by the look on Bam's face. Once he was pissed off, nobody could tell him anything. He'd been that way since he was a little kid.

Terri said, "It look like Bam 'bout to get his man. Latif better chill the fuck out."

"I hope Jay break that shit up before it get outta' hand," Lisa said. "You know Latif fire that pistol. He'll shoot Bam wit' no questions asked. I'd hate to see it."

I was hoping Jay would defuse the situation as well. It was a known fact that Bam didn't give a fuck about who Latif was supposed to be nor the fact that Latif had killed a nigga before. Bam was one of those young niggaz who just didn't bow down to anybody, even if it could cost him his life.

"Damn!" Terri shouted, her eyes wide with excitement and surprise.

Out the corner of my eyes, I saw it all go down. Bam swung a mean left hook and knocked Latif out cold. Latif hit the ground, face first. He was lying there motionless. All I could do was shake my head. Everybody was trying to grab Bam as he stomped Latif.

Lisa said, "It look like he knocked out, y'all."

"He is. He fucked up," I said.

Finally, Jay got Bam off of Latif and tried to calm him down while Troy checked on Latif. Police sirens hit the air. Bam and his crew took off running. They hit the alley and disappeared.

Lisa started the truck. "Let's get the fuck outta' here. It's time to go. That nigga might be dead."

I said, "No bullshit."

We pulled off just as the police were bending the corner.

* * *

Later on, Jay came over to my apartment to holla at me. He needed me to take another trip to New York. I was down. That was another quick $2,000 to throw in the stash. I had plans. Getting my mother a good lawyer to get her out of prison was first on the list.

"This time I need you to take some money up there to give to Twin for me. Cool?"

"How much money?" I said, raising my eyebrow

"Eighty-five thousand," Jay said as he turned the TV to ESPN.

"That's a lot of paper. What if somethin' happens? What if I get robbed or somethin'?" I was a little nervous about carrying close to $100,000 in cash with me on the train to New York. In D.C., young niggaz were robbing people for shit as frivolous as cell phones and iPods. I was sure I could get robbed for $85,000. I didn't want to be responsible for Jay's money.

Jay put his hand on my shoulder and said, "Don't worry about that, Niya. Ain't nothin' gon' happen to you. You gon' be fine. I wouldn't put you in no bad situation. Just work your little college look, and it'll all good, baby girl."

I shrugged. "Okay, I'm wit' it."

"Check this out though," he said, rubbing his chin. "Instead of three joints, Twin gon' give you five this time. Cool?"

"I can handle that."

Jay smiled, rubbed my back, and said, "Good girl. You a muthafuckin' soldier. I'ma make sure you get your paper right. I got you, I promise."

"I feel you. You know what's good with me. All I really want to do is get my moms out of prison."

"I feel you on that. I can help you do that. What's the deal wit' your mother's case? What you need to do to get her out?"

"I'm not sure right now. I'm tryin' to look into a lawyer for her right now. I'll let you know somethin' as soon as I find out."

"Cool. Just let me know and I will do whatever." Jay brushed my hair out of my face with his hand and looked at the scratches Tish left on my forehead. The scratches didn't look that bad, but I was still letting my hair hang down over them to cover them up. "Tish scratched you up a little bit, huh?"

"It ain't nothin'. You already know I beat that ass. A few scratches ain't shit. You shoulda seen her ass on the ground balled up like a bitch. Fuck her."

Jay laughed. "I saw her today. She fucked up, for real. She got two black eyes and her nose broke. The joint set in a splint. She lookin' real bad, like she was in a car accident or some shit."

I laughed. I didn't feel bad at all. Tish deserved all she got. She needed to learn some respect. "I bet she stay the fuck out of my business now."

"I bet you she do too," he laughed.

"What's up wit' that shit wit' Bam and Latif?"

Jay sighed and shook his head. "Man, that was some wild shit there. I tried to dead it, but you know how Bam is. When he got his mind set, it ain't nothin' you can tell that young nigga. It just ain't no talkin' to him. I told Latif he can't be talkin' that gangsta shit to them youngins. Bam don't be stuntin' none of that shit. I fucks wit' both of them, but it ain't too much I can do about that shit now. Bam embarrassed Latif. He hurt his pride, so it's gon' be some shit behind that there. You know that. When a nigga's pride is hurt, ain't no tellin' what he'll do. I'm out of that shit, Niya. I feel sorry for whoever gets the short end of the stick."

I shook my head. "What was all that shit about?"

"Latif was jokin', talkin' 'bout he used to send Bam to the store for him when Bam was a little nigga. Bam wasn't feelin' that shit. He told Latif to stop playin' wit' him or he was gon' knock his ass out. Latif wasn't feelin' what Bam was talkin' about and told Bam he'd beat his ass. They started arguing and Bam stole his ass, knocked him out cold. I couldn't believe it. It happened so fast."

I shook my head. "That's fucked up." I was concerned how things would play out. I didn't want anything to happen to Bam. "Ain't no way you can squash that shit?"

Jay laughed. "How? Bam knocked Latif out in front of everybody. Ain't too much I can do or say. It's out of my hands now."

I understood where Jay was coming from.

Jay looked at his watch and said, "I gotta go meet Troy. I'ma catch you later. Be ready to make that trip tomorrow, around twelve. Cool?"

"No problem."

Jay left.

I thought about what I felt like doing for the night and told myself that I felt like hitting the club in style. Lisa and Terri wanted to hit Club Uptown. Lil Wayne was supposed to be in the spot. My hair and my nails were fresh, I had fresh gear, and I was pushing the Range. I felt like I might as well go out for a second and have some fun. I hadn't been out in a while.

One-Night Stand

Club Uptown was packed from wall to wall. Big boys were inside the joint. I mean niggaz who were gettin' real paper. Rappers and ball players were rubbing shoulders with regular street niggaz. I hit the second floor with Lisa and Terri. We were killing the game, dressed to impress by all means. I was doing my Roberto Cavalli thing and carrying a Valentino bag. We were getting so much attention it had me feeling like a super star. It felt good. I needed to have some fun.

As we passed L.A. Lakers forward Lamar Odom, Terri said, "Everbody up in this muthafucka tonight. I saw the nigga Reggie Bush downstairs. I might catch me a nigga wit' some real paper in here."

Club Uptown was owned by a dude named Corky from First and Kennedy. It was on Georgia Avenue, right by the Maryland line. From what I could see, Corky had done a nice job on the place.

Lisa said, "I'm feelin' this joint. Glad we got in free 'cause I wasn't about to pay no $75 to get in here."

We all laughed as we made our way through the crowd. We found our little chill spot on a sofa in the back. Before I knew it, dudes were all over us, trying to buy us drinks and shit. Lisa loved that kind of shit. She got a dude to get us two bottles of Moet Imperial Rose. We started sipping our drinks and having a good time. I started feeling nice. The music was sounding better the more I sipped. Shit, I was feeling sexier the more I sipped too.

Lisa said, "Ay, Niya, ain't that your little friend Face over there?" She pointed at a group of dudes behind us.

I looked to see if she knew what she was talking about. Face was talking to some dudes who looked like they were important. They had on diamonds and top-of-the-line gear. Fly as shit. Either paid street niggaz or music industry niggaz. One of the two.

I turned back to my girls and said, "Yeah, that's Face."

Terri said, "Niya, you ain't tell me you had a friend."

I knew what was on Terri's mind. Face was looking fly as shit, without the diamonds. He had swagger like he was getting money.

I had told Lisa about my thing with Face, but I never got a chance to holla at Terri about it.

I smiled at Terri and said, "He's just a friend of mine, Terri. That's all."

She gave me that "don't bullshit me" look. "Just a friend, huh? Yeah, right."

I laughed. So did Lisa.

"So what's his story?" she asked. "He gettin' paper?"

"He ain't in the game. He work and make music, shit like that. He good peoples, though." I smiled. It felt funny telling her I was talking to a dude who made music. It's not like he was Kanye West or somebody. Nevertheless, he was cool with me.

Terri laughed. "Get the fuck outt' here, Niya. He make music? Like beats and shit?"

I wasn't feeling the fact that she was laughing. She was rubbing me the wrong way, but I played it cool. I said, "Go 'head wit' that bullshit."

She was dying laughing, holding her stomach like it was hurting her.

Lisa smiled. She was holding back her laugh out of respect for me.

"Hold up, hold up, hold the fuck up," Terri said, still laughing. She put her hand up like, wait a minute! "He makes beats like Dr. Dre or somebody?"

I rolled my eyes. I had to laugh myself, though.

Lisa knew I would snap, so she said, "Go 'head, Terri, don't make her mad."

"Okay, my bad. I was just havin' fun." She tried to stop laughing. "I thought you was into street niggaz, though."

I smiled. "Fuck you, ho. Face cool as shit, plus his tongue game on one thousand." We all laughed. "But on the real, he cool peoples. I fucks wit' him."

Lisa sipped her drink and said, "He comin' this way, Niya."

I looked back and locked eyes with Face. A smile crossed my face. He had a sexy smile on his face.

Thoughts of our night together made my pussy tingle. His dreads were pulled back in a ponytail. He had on a Gucci shirt and some blue jeans with some slick-ass Prada shoes. He stepped to me and said, "You lookin' real good tonight, Niya."

"Thank you." I smiled as I got up to give him a hug.

Lisa and Terri looked like they wanted to laugh, but they didn't. They couldn't hate. Face was looking good as shit.

Face spoke to them. They spoke back. He then asked to speak to me alone. We stepped off for a second.

Face put his arms around me and kissed me like I was his girl. I was cool with it. I was feeling him more and more.

Face said, "Guess what, Niya."

I smiled. The Rose had me feeling real good. "What's up, Face?"

"I just ran into this dude named Stone. He own a record label called South Side Records. He bought a few beats before. He say one of his artist 'bout to drop a album, and two of my tracks gon' be on the joint. He want me to go down Atlanta wit' them next week to work on some shit in the studio for the album. He gon' pay me, plus I'ma make money off the album for the work I put in." Excitement was in his eyes. I could tell he was looking forward to this move.

I was happy for him, happy about his apparent come-up. I knew it was what he had been working so hard for. I smiled and hugged him. "I'm proud of you, boy."

"Thanks. That means a lot to me."

I gave him a sexy smile. He gave me a tight hug and squeezed my ass. He said, "You my boo, girl." He said that with confidence. I liked that.

I smiled. "You my boo, too. You gon' do big things. I know it."

"I'ma make this shit work, and I'ma treat you good when I get on."

"Awww, I like that. You so sweet, Face." I couldn't stop blushing. "You ain't runnin' game is you?"

He smiled. "Never that. I'm feelin' you. Believe that."

"You say all the right things. I give you that."

"It is what it is, Niya."

"I believe you. So what you got planned for the night?"

"The dude Stone want me to hit the VIP wit' him and his peoples so he can introduce me to the artist he want me to work wit' down Atlanta."

"I see you steppin' up in the world, huh?" I joked. "You bet' not forget about me when you get on either."

He kissed me. "Never that, boo."

A second later, a half-dressed ho with her ass hanging out walked by and told Face that the dude Stone was waiting for him in VIP. I looked her up and down like she had a bad smell coming from her face. I told Face to take care of his business and that I would holla at him later.

As he left, Face whispered, "Don't be so mean, Niya. I don't want her."

"Act like you know then," I said as I stepped off.

Face smiled as he headed toward the VIP.

I rejoined my girls.

Terri smirked as she sipped her drink. She "Just a friend, huh, Niya?" she said.

"Y'all was real friendly over there, Niya. No bullshit," Lisa added.

I took a sip of my drink and said, "I told yall I'm feeling Face. What can I say? I ain't gon' fake like I don't feel him."

Terri said, "I know that's right. Do you, girl. I see your friend hit the VIP wit' them South Side niggaz. That nigga Stone got that big-boy money, that Big Meech money, girl."

Lisa said, "BMF, Big Meech?"

"Hell yeah! You ain't hip to him? He just beat some big drug case. *The Washington Post* said that he was one of the biggest drug dealers D.C. has seen in the last fifteen years. He's the real deal, I'm tellin' you."

I said, "Get the fuck outta here, for real?"

"I bullshit you not. Stone and them makin' some serious cake in the streets. They got that Alabama Avenue end on lock. They got family in the Farms, Parkland, Condon Terrace, all that shit. That record label shit is just a front. Where you bitches been?"

Terri kept up with all that kind of shit. It's what she was into. She was like a walking *Don Diva* magazine. She knew what was what and who was who in the streets of D.C. Her ear was always to the streets.

Lisa sounded tipsy when she said, "Well, Face might got more goin' for himself than we really know. It be like that sometimes.

"I doubt it," I said. "He ain't into all that street shit. He just wanna' get on wit' his music. The dude

Stone probably see somethin' in him. He knew Face like that wit' that music shit, so he want him on his team."

Terri said, "Hell yeah, they tryin' to get they foot in the door wit' that music shit, so if Face is like you say he is, then they want him on the team. That makes sense. They tryin' to clean that money."

As the night went on, we drank and laughed and had an all around good time. On the real, I missed hanging out with my girls.

A little while later, Jay and Troy, along with a few other dudes from around Rittenhouse Street, came through the door looking like new money. They saw us and made their way over. They always fucked with us when they saw us out at a club or something. Since we were all homies, they felt the need to sweat us when they ran into us. Like always, Troy was trying to holla at me, although he was doing it in a joking way. The bottom line was that he wanted some pussy. Jay was rappin' to Terri and Lisa—he could get away with that. Either one would give him the pussy. There was no doubt in my mind about that. I didn't think Jay would really fuck with either one of them for real. He was just enjoying flirting with them both. I'm sure the thought of being able to fuck them both didsomething real big for his ego.

Jay said, "I'ma get some more bottles." He stepped off and returned with more bottles of Rose. "Don't say I don't show love."

Lisa and Terri laughed as they gave each other high fives. Lisa said, "Okay, homie love. That's what it's all about."

We all laughed.

Troy passed around some E pills. I was feeling good, so I popped one. Fuck it, I was out to have fun.

Lil Wayne hit the stage a short while later. He did his thing. I was feeling him.

By this time, the E pills had me highly sensitive and feeling sexy as shit. I was dancing as Lil Wayne performed. I was feeling so good I had lost track of what was going on around me. I turned around and saw Jay arguing with one of Stone's peoples—the dude had on a South Side T-shirt. Out of the blue, Troy smashed a bottle of Rose over the dude's head, knocking him to the ground.

"Oh, shit!" I said out loud as all hell broke loose. Motherfuckers came from every direction. Niggaz who were rolling with Jay rushed to the scene. South Side niggaz who were rolling with Stone did the same. The two groups collided like speeding trains on the same track. Punches and chairs were being thrown. Security rushed the scene. Bottles of Rose and Ace of Spades were bashed over heads. People were screaming, trying to get the fuck out of the way. I came to my senses real quick and headed for the door, almost getting caught in the melee.

Terri grabbed my arm as I fought my way through the crowd, trying to get out of the door. "Girl we gotta get the fuck outta here before the guns come out. Somebody gon' get fucked around tonight!" Terri said.

I followed behind Lisa and Terri as we forced our way outside, onto Georgia Avenue.

* * *

Outside, I got separated from Lisa and Terri as we got caught up in the crowd that was being directed down the street by D.C. police. My heart told me that it was going to be some shooting. I could feel it in my bones, and I didn't want to be around when the bullets started flying. I made it to the Range and jumped behind the wheel quickly. My heart was racing a mile a minute as I fumbled with the keys. Gunshots rang out, making me jump. They were somewhere close — too close. I wasn't trying to catch a stray. More gunshots went off. Scared the shit out of me. People were running for their lives down Georgia Avenue. Gunshots kept going off. Fully automatic shit. They sounded closer and closer with every second. I ducked my head and prayed I didn't get hit. *Fuck!* I dropped my keys on the dark floor. My cell phone went off. Too much was going on at one time. My heart was racing like someone was chasing me.

Somebody banged on my driver's side window as more gunshots tore through the night. Police sirens were in the air. It sounded like they were coming from everywhere. "Open the door!" someone yelled.

Nervous, I looked up and saw Jay. I opened the door quickly. He jumped inside, looking over his shoulder at what was going on down the street. In a rush, he said, "Let me drive."

We switched places with the quickness. He started the truck and pulled into traffic as police cars flew by us with their sirens blaring. Jay wasted no time. He drove on the sidewalk and flew down the street and around the corner at top speed. I struggled to put on my seatbelt. After running through countless stop signs, we hit Blair Road. Jay kept looking over his shoulder like he expected someone to be behind us.

My phone went off again. I looked at the screen and answered the phone. "Lisa, you okay? Where are you?"

"Yeah, I'm okay, I'm good. Where you at? I was worried about you."

"I'm good. I'm wit' Jay. Where Terri at?"

"She wit' me. We headed down Georgia Avenue, headed home. Shit outta control back there. A nigga was layin' dead in the middle of the street, brains all out and everything. Shit was crazy."

"I know, right? I got the fuck outta there too. I'll call you when I get in the house."

"Okay, do that."

I ended the call.

Jay looked pissed off. His jaw was clenched, and he was gripping the wheel like he wanted to break it.

"Are you okay? Is everything alright? What was all that about back there?"

Jay shook his head. "Nothing." He said that like he didn't want to talk about whatever it was.

I shrugged it off. I knew he would talk about when he was ready.

Jay's phone went off. He answered it quickly. From the sound of things, it had to be Troy. That meant that Troy was safe or at least alive. That was good. After a hot second on the phone, Jay ended the call.

We crossed North Capitol Street and headed into Northeast, D.C. I had no idea where we were going, but we sure weren't headed back around the way. "Where we goin', Jay?" ·

"I gotta get my car. I rode to the club wit' Troy and them."

"Jay, what the hell is going on?"

He cut his eyes at me in a way that told me he was irritated.

"I thought you trusted me."

He cracked a slight smile. "I do trust you, Niya."

"Well why you actin' like you don't want to tell me what the fuck is goin' on? I don't run my mouth. Shit, I seen you smoke a nigga before, and I ain't say shit about it when the feds questioned me. If you can't trust me, who can you trust?"

"You right, baby girl." He cracked the window to get some air. "One of them South Side Records niggaz owe me some change. He think 'cause he under the nigga Stone I won't punish his ass about my paper. Little do he know I don't give a fuck about him or Stone. It could be George Bush for all I care. I don't play no games about mine. Feel me?"

"I feel you." I understood.

A short while later we ended up at an apartment complex in Temple Hills, MD. Jay's 350 ZX was in the parking lot, parked in front of the last building. He pulled up and parked beside it.

"So what you 'bout to do now?" I was still tipsy and rollin' off the E.

"I'm 'bout to change clothes and meet Troy uptown. Why? What's good?"

"I'm too tipsy to be drivin' back uptown this late at night."

"I got an apartment out here. You wanna spend the night?"

I thought about it for a second. "Yeah, that's cool. Thanks."

We headed inside and went up to the second floor, where one of his apartments was. It wasn't much inside. Just a TV on the floor in the living room and a sofa. The joint had to be a stash house.

I smiled and said, "You ain't got much furniture up in here, huh?"

"I got food in the fridge and a bed in the bedroom. I don't need much here. Make yourself at home." He smiled. "The sheets clean. Get some rest. I'm 'bout to change clothes real quick."

I followed him to the bedroom. It was nothing in the bedroom but a bed. Jay went to the closet to get a change of clothes. He had a few clothes hanging up in there. A safe was on the floor, an AK-47 assault rifle was leaning against the back wall. A large banana clip was in the AK. I sat on the bed and took my shoes off. I just wanted to lie down.

"Ay, Jay," I said.

"Yeah," he said as he took off his shirt.

"Who got shot?"

He turned and faced me. He gave me a firm look and said, "One of them South Side niggaz." He threw on a dark blue Polo T-shirt and then took off his jeans. Standing there in his boxers he rubbed his chin as if he were in deep thought. "Get some rest, Niya. Don't forget I need you to make that trip for me tomorrow." He turned around and grabbed another pair of jeans.

"Okay, I got you." My cell phone went off. It was Face. I really didn't want to speak to Face in front of Jay for some reason. I let the call go to voice mail. I'd call him back later.

Jay pulled a huge pistol from under the bed and popped a clip in it. He slid another clip in his pocket before he hit the road. "I'm gone, Niya. See you tomorrow." He left without another word.

I put my phone in my purse and lay down. As soon Jay left and locked the door behind himself, my cell phone went off again. "What's up, Lisa?"

"Niya, where you at?!" She sounded excited and worried at the same time.

I really didn't know how to answer her question. I didn't want her to know that I was at Jay's apartment. She would swear I was fucking him. "I'm over a friend's house. What's good? Why you sound like that? You okay?"

"Latif shot Bam and Lil Quan! Police all over the place. They was puttin' Bam in the ambulance. I think he fucked up bad. They already had a white sheet over Lil Quan. That's fucked up, Niya. Latif ain't have to do that like—I"

I cut her off. "Stop kickin' all them names on my phone, Lisa. Talk to me when you see me."

"My bad, my bad, I'm trippin'. But that's fucked up. On everything! Plus his dumb ass did that bamma shit in front of everybody."

I shook my head. I knew some shit was going to come behind the whole situation between Bam and Latif. I just wished that Bam wouldn't have gotten the short end of the stick. I felt sorry for Bam and Lil Quan. Lil Quan was only 15. I hoped Bam would pull through. At this point, I knew that shit was going to get ugly around the way. It was definitely going to be a hot summer. All the young niggaz were going to be beefin' with the older niggaz around the way.

"Did Bam get shot bad?"

"Bam got hit a few times in the chest—I think it was the chest. Quan got hit in the face, though. It was terrible. The feds was talkin' like Bam ain't gon' make it. This shit is crazy, Niya."

I sighed and shook my head. "I knew that shit was gon' happen."

"Bam just came home too." Lisa sounded like she was about to cry.

"I know. Shit fucked up," I said. My phone beeped. It was Face calling again. "Lisa, I gotta take this call. I'll holla at you tomorrow."

"Okay, talk to you later."

I clicked over. "What's up, Face?"

"You okay, Niya?"

I smiled. "Yeah, I'm okay. Thanks for asking. You good?"

"Yeah, I'm good. I was concerned about you. That's the only reason I called. I was lookin' for you outside the club and couldn't find you."

"I had to get the hell out of there. I don't hang around when the bullets start flyin'. They ain't got no names on 'em. Where you at?"

"Home. Wish I was wit' you, though."

He made me blush. The sound of his voice alone turned me on. He sounded like he desired me, and that made me wet with ease. The E pill still had me feeling nice and horny. "I wish I was with you too."

"We can make that happen, sexy. Just say the word."

I laughed. "Maybe another time. I need to get some rest, boo. I got some business to take care of tomorrow."

"Okay, Niya, I'ma let you get some rest."

"What happened when you went up to the VIP section to holla at the dude Stone?Everything go well?"

"Yeah, it's all good. I'ma go down Atlanta next week. Shit should work out real good if all goes well. We was supposed to talk about some money before niggaz started fightin' and shit."

From the way Face was talking, I figured he didn't know that one of the South Side dudes got shot. I wasn't going to bring it up either, not on my phone.

"I wish you the best, Face. I know you gon' make it do what it do. I'll call you tomorrow."

"Catch you then, Niya. Sleep well."

"You too."

When I got off the phone with Face, I went in the kitchen and got a glass of ice water. I was thirsty as shit. I took my water back to the bedroom and sat on the bed. I was still feeling good. The alcohol and E had me thinking about going to see Face, but there was no way I was making that trip all the way uptown. I finished the water and pushed that thought out of my mind, even though the way Face ate pussy had me thinking about taking the trip.

I needed a shower. I found towels and wash cloths in the closet, so I undressed and headed to the bathroom. The hot water felt good against my sensitive skin. I washed my body and my nipples grew hard. I thought about Face as I washed my legs. I kept thinking about him eating my pussy. Those thoughts made my pussy tingle.

When I got out of the shower, I wrapped my body in a thick towel and headed back to the bedroom. I screamed as soon as I stepped foot in the bedroom. I almost had a damn heart attack. Jay was standing in the bedroom making a call on his cell phone.

He smiled and said, "It's just me, Niya. Don't trip, baby girl."

"You scared the shit out of me, boy. When did you come back in here?" I said, holding my heart. "You need to make some noise next time."

He laughed.

"What's so damn funny? You scared the shit out of me for real, Jay. If I had a gun, I woulda' shot your ass." I rolled my eyes.

"Calm down. Ain't nothin' gon' happen to you in my joint. You safe here."

I headed back to the bathroom. Over my shoulder, I said, "I thought you was goin' back uptown."

"I was, but it's hot as shit around the way. Bam and Lil Quan got shot. They say—"

"I heard." I went back into the bedroom and sat on the bed in nothing but my towel.

"Damn, you keep your ear to the streets, don't you?"

"Lisa told me. That's fucked up."

Jay shrugged. "I knew that shit was gon' get ugly. It wasn't shit I could do about it."

I shook my head.

"Fuck that shit. Go 'head and get yourself together. I'ma roll some smoke real quick." He left the room and shut the door behind him.

I dried off, looked in the closet and threw on a long black Polo T-shirt. I grabbed my bra and panties, took them to the bathroom, and threw them in the washer with a little Tide. When I came out of the bathroom, Jay was sitting on the floor in the living room watching *Paid In Full,* smoking a Backwood with his pistol beside him.

He looked at me and said, "Wanna hit this?"

I nodded, walked over, and took the Backwood out of his hand. I took a few hits and passed it back.

Jay laughed.

"What?" I asked.

"You look cute in my T-shirt." He rubbed the back of my leg. That sent chills through my body. It surprised me and turned me on at the same time. I stepped back and looked into his eyes. He looked at my lustfully, passionately. He wanted to fuck me. It was written all over his face. However, that wasn't what surprised me. What surprised me was the fact that I was feeling the same way: I wanted him to fuck me. It had to be the E and the alcohol and weed that had me feeling such a way.

"Stop playin', Jay."

"I ain't playin'. You lookin' sexy as shit."

I was horny. I wasn't thinking straight. I was rolling off the pill.

Jay hit the Backwood one hard time and stood up. He said, "Come here, baby girl."

I did.

He turned the Backwood around and put the lit part in his mouth. With his fingers he signaled for me to come closer. I did. Face to face, we were close enough to kiss. He blew me a shotgun. I sucked the weed smoke into my lungs as he blew it in my mouth. Weed smoke gushed out of the Backwood like an exhaust pipe. The effects hit me hard and fast, had me high as shit and feeling good.

Jay gave me the Backwood and said, "Blow me a gun."

I did him like he did me and blew the weed into his mouth. As I blew the shotgun, I felt his hands on my breasts. More chills went through my body. *Oh my God,* I thought. My nipples were hard as bullets. He squeezed my nipples between his thumbs and index fingers. I felt like I was going to cum on myself if he kept it up. I took the Backwood out of my mouth and said, "What are you doin', Jay?"

"Let me show you what I'm doin'." He took the Backwood, hit it a few times, and threw it in the kitchen sink.

I was stuck. Lust and desire were taking over. I was feeling overly sexual. The whole situation was wrong, and I knew it, but it was feeling so right at the time. I was getting wetter with every passing second.

Again, Jay looked at me like he couldn't resist me. I wanted to stop what was going on between us. Yet the wetter I got, the more my rationale ran away from me. Jay rubbed my shoulders. It felt good. I didn't resist him this time. He sent more chills through my body. Slowly, looking into my eyes, Jay pulled me close to him. I felt so weak, so helpless. He could do anything he wanted to me. I couldn't resist. He kissed me. Damn, his lips were so soft. I rubbed his back and pressed my body against his. My breasts and hard nipples pressed against his hard chest. His tongue felt so smooth as it moved inside my mouth. My inner thighs were so wet at this point. My breathing was getting heavy. I looked Jay in the eyes as we kissed, and all I could think about was how he would feel inside me. Rubbing his hands down my back, Jay went under the T-shirt and grabbed my ass. He squeezed it hard. I could feel him growing hard against my body.

There was no turning back at this point.

Jay said, "I want to get in that pussy, Niya."

I closed my eyes, shook my head, and covered his lips with my finger. "No ... don't talk ... let's not talk," I whispered. I didn't want to talk about what we were doing, didn't even want to think about what we were doing. All I wanted to do was feel what we were doing.

With my ass firmly in his grip, Jay pulled me closer to him, grinding his hardness against me. I was dripping wet at this point; I could feel it easing down my thighs. He inhaled me, took a deep breath, took in my freshness. He licked my neck, then began sucking it. I reached for his pants, undid them and eased my hand inside. I felt his hardness. Next, I felt his finger slide inside my pussy from the back. In and out, long, slow movements. I closed my eyes and moaned softly. Oh, God, it felt so good.

I pulled away from Jay. He looked at me with surprise. I walked to the bedroom, pulling the T-shirt over my head and dropping it on the carpeted floor. I climbed in the bed and rolled onto my back. Jay followed right behind me, undressing. He climbed into the bed and grabbed my breasts, rubbing them. His erection was strong and proud, ready for whatever. My eyes were glued to his dick. It seemed like I was losing track of time as he rubbed his hands all over me. His touch felt so good against my skin. All I could feel was pleasure and ecstasy as he took control of me. He kissed me. I felt his finger slip back into my pussy. He squeezed and rubbed my clit with his fingers. That sent more chills through my body. I arched my back, and my eyes rolled back in my head. I pulled the sheets in every direction. Jay kissed all the way down to my pussy. He licked my clit in circles and then up and down. It felt so good. He started sucking my clit. It was driving me crazy, had me trying to get away from him. He began to lick figure eights around my clit.

"Mmmmmm ... don't stop," I moaned. I grabbed his head with my hands as he ate my pussy. I grinded my pussy against his face; I just couldn't get enough.

Before I knew it, he had me doggy style, sliding in and out of me. He had me moaning for more. With every passing second he fucked me harder, like he was trying to prove a point. It was so good. He was crushing the pussy, but I took it like a big girl. I didn't want him to stop. I threw it back like a pro. I wanted more of what he was giving. He smacked my ass. That too sent chills through my body. I began throwing it back harder; I was loving what he was doing to me. After digging in me for a while, he slowed it down and started long-stroking me. Hit my spot with ease. I felt like I was about to cum.

I moaned, "Oh shit ... I'm cummin', Jay. Oh, my God, Jay! I'm cummin' ... oh my God!" I exploded. I couldn't remember ever cumming that hard before. Jay was a monster. He was fucking the shit out of me like it was nothing. I couldn't believe how good he was making me feel. Still cumming, I moaned, "Fuck me … fuck me, don't stop, Jay … fuck the shit outta this pussy." He was fucking me hard and deep, pulling me back to him with force and aggression, just the way I liked it.

I was in another world. I moaned, "Oh, God, yes … yes, yes ... don't stop! You're so fuckin' deep."

Jay grunted, stroke for stroke, "You-like-that-huh? You-like-that? You-like-the-way-I'm-fuckin'-you?!"

"Oh, God … shiiiit!" I shouted.

He sped up. He fucked me faster, like he was in a race. I was close to another orgasm. Faster. Harder. Deeper. He fucked the shit out of me.

He grunted, "You so damn tight, Niya, I can't …" He pulled out of me and shot warm cum all over my back and ass. It felt good. I whimpered and wanted him back inside of me.

"Ahhhh …" I moaned as he continued to explode.

Out of breath, we collapsed.

Jay looked at me and whispered, "Your pussy is so good girl."

I smiled and shook my head. I couldn't believe what we'd just done.

Back to Business

The next morning I woke up around 11:30. Jay was already up, sitting on the edge of the bed in his boxers. He was talking on his cell phone, with his back to me. I could tell that he was talking to Troy. The conversation was intense. They weren't seeing eye to eye about something.

I rolled over on my side and faced the window. It was raining outside; the sky was dark and gray. Rubbing my eyes, I tried to collect my thoughts. I couldn't believe what we had done last night. I could still feel him inside me. What we did last night was wrong. I knew it was wrong, and I didn't stop it. Jay didn't stop it either. Even though it felt good, it was still wrong. I felt guilt in my heart. I tried to make sense of it in my mind. I couldn't. I blamed it on the E, the weed, the alcohol. I even blamed it on Jay. But I had to take some of the blame. I played a major role in the whole damn thing. Deep down inside, I wanted to be with Jay at least once. Now we had crossed the line, and there was nothing we could do to change that.

No longer high or under the influence of alcohol, I felt a serious awkwardness as a I lay in Jay's bed, naked. I took a deep breath and shook my head at the whole situation.

Jay ended his phone call and looked over his shoulder at me. We said nothing for a second, just looked at one another. It seemed like we were thinking same thing. Jay had a serious look in his eyes. He said, "I know what you thinkin'."

"What? What am I thinkin', Jay?"

"You second-guessin' what we did. You feel like we did somethin' wrong, don't you?"

I sighed in agreement.

"We did what we did, Niya. It is what it is. It was what we felt at the time." He shrugged and continued, "You okay wit' it?"

"No, not really. I mean ... I don't know. I mean, you was Jaz's man ..."

With an understanding nod he said, "I know. I feel you. I don't want to sound cold or like I don't care. I loved Jaz. That was my baby, but she's gone now, Niya. At the same time, I feel somethin' for you, and it all came to a head last night. I couldn't fake like I didn't want you. You had to feel the same way. Am I right?"

I nodded in agreement. He was right. I knew he was right. I had to admit that to myself. Guilt was still eating away at me.

Silence fell between us for a second.

"You know what, Niya? We can do it like this: We can act like it didn't happen, or we can try to make sense of it. It's up to you, baby girl."

I smiled half-heartedly and shook my head. "It did happen, Jay. Ain't no gettin' around that. The only way to make sense of it is to accept what happened. We had sex. Simple as that."

He nodded. "We did. We had sex. I'm cool wit' that. Ain't nothin' else to it. It's between me and you."

"Cool," I said, wanting to change the subject.

"Let me ask you one more thing."

"What?" I said.

"Did you enjoy it?"

I smiled and shook my head. "Are you serious, boy?"

"On everything, did you enjoy it? Was it worth it?"

I nodded. "It was a'ight," I joked.

He laughed.

"I came so hard. I was lovin' it."

"It was worth it then. Would you do it again?"

"One time thing, boo." I smiled. "I can't get down like that without the guilt killin' me. I'm gon' always see you as Jaz's man."

"I feel you. It's all good."

"We still cool peoples. I don't want this to change nothin' between us, though."

"It's all good, Niya. Ain't nothin' gon' change between us. Believe that."

"Cool," I smiled.

"Well, on another note, I still need you to make that trip for me."

"I know. I'm 'bout to get up and get in the shower."

He leaned over and kissed me on the forehead. "I fucks wit' you, girl." He got up and headed to the bathroom.

* * *

The Amtrak train headed North. I was on my way to New York with $85,000 in a Polo backpack. I was working my little college girl look. No one was paying me any attention as I sat alone reading *The Washington Post* and listening to Tabi Bonney on my iPod. There was a small article in the Metro section of the paper about the shooting around my way. The article didn't say much, but it did mention that Bam got shot pretty bad and that Lil Quan got killed. According to the *Post*, a gunman opened fire on the two juveniles, killing one, and then fled north on Georgia Avenue.

There was also an article about the shooting at Club Uptown. It said an altercation inside the club between two rival groups led to a shootout outside the club moments later and that a 24-year-old man was pronounced dead at the scene. His name was being withheld until his family was notified. Nothing else in the paper held my attention. I folded it up and stuffed it inside my backpack. I pulled out my Wahida Clark book, *Every Thug Needs a Lady*, and dug into it.

Before I knew it, I was in New York. I had just finished the last few chapters of my novel. I stuffed it into my backpack and got my mind right. I had to be on point. Just like the last time, I called Jay as soon as I got off the train. "I'm at Penn Station."

"Good girl. Stay on point and it's all good."

"Okay."

"Go 'head and jump in a cab. I'ma' call Twin and let him know you on your way. Handle your business."

"I got you." I ended the call and headed uptown.

The cab ride through the New York traffic took forever, but I made it to Harlem in good time. The Arab cab driver was acting like a bitch. He didn't want to wait for me, even though I told him I would give him an extra $50. I wanted to cuss his ass out, but I couldn't stand any unwanted attention. I left it alone.

St. Nicholas Avenue was full of life; people were all over the place. Just like last time, a few dudes were standing in front of Twin's building. They all had that Harlem swagger. Twin's man, Black, recognized me from the last time. He nodded at me. I nodded back.

"What's up, ma?" he said.

"I'm good." I looked up and down the busy street as I headed for the building. It was hot as hell outside. I was in a hurry to get inside the apartment.

Black led me inside the building. All eyes were on me, but I could tell the dudes in front of the building now had an idea that I was about business. I didn't have time for bullshit, and I wasn't in New York to meet any new friends.

Inside the elevator, Black said, "Ay, ma, I ain't tryin' to get in your businss, but can I ask you a question?"

I looked at Black and studied his eyes. I didn't know where he was coming from but I said, "Depends on the question, champ."

He smiled. "True, true, I respect that. But, uh, ain't you kinda young to be … uh … movin' like you movin'?"

I snickered. "I'm old enough."

He nodded and left it like that.

Too many questions were never a good thing.

We made it to Twin's spot on the 14th floor, and Black knocked on the door. Just like last time, Twin opened the door. He smiled and said, "What's good, D.C.?"

"It's all good. What's up wit' you?"

"Good. All is well." He let me in and told Black to wait in the hall. He shut the door so we could get down to business.

The same brown-skin girl from last time, the one Twin called Goldie, was sitting on the sofa looking at a *Don Diva* magazine with MS-13 on the cover. The TV was on BET. A Young Jeezy video was going off. She looked at me with curious eyes. I looked at her the same way. For some reason, Goldie looked familiar. I'd seen her somewhere before, but I couldn't put my finger on it. We exchanged nods, and that was that.

Twin said, "Goldie, grab them joints you wrapped up for me, baby."

Goldie, dressed in booty shorts and a gray T-shirt, headed for the back room.

Looking at me with his ever-present smile, Twin said, "D.C., have a seat. I wanna run somethin' by you, ma."

Twin sat next to me and said, "I spoke to Jay about you. He speaks very highly of you. I told him that I'm feelin' your style. You know how to carry yourself. That's rare these days. Anyway ... I got a proposition for you. Jay said it was cool to run it by you."

Goldie came back in the living room carrying a brown shopping bag. Twin told her to sit the bag on the floor by him. She did just that and disappeared into the back room to let us talk. She knew her place well.

I looked at Twin and said, "What's the proposition?"

"I got some things going on in B-more, Richmond, and D.C. Some nice things. I'm lookin' for somebody with brains, looks, and the balls to drop some work off for me. Somebody that knows how to keep shit to theyself. The money is sweet. I think you would be perfect for the job."

I thought about the money being sweet. I was all about making some paper. I raised my eyebrows and said, "What kind of money you talkin'?"

"Five thousand a trip. Money up front. I pay for all the expenses."

I saw dollar signs. "Five thousand, huh?"

"Yeah, like I said, money up front. You can't beat that."

"How much work you need dropped off?" I asked.

"Depends on where it's goin'. Ten bricks, maybe fifteen, sometimes twenty."

"Wow, that's a lot of work." That sounded like a life sentence to me. I really wasn't feeling the move. How the fuck was I going to move twenty bricks of coke? It wasn't like I could throw that amount of coke in my backpack and hop on the train with it.

Twin smiled and said, "I know it sounds like a lot of coke, but it ain't what it seems. This is how it works: You'll get a car or a truck that's already loaded wit' the work. It will be hid in compartments that you couldn't find if you tore the car up. You'll be good, I promise. That's my word. All you gotta do is drive the car to the location and somebody else will take it from there. Simple as that. You pocket five Gs just like that.

Yeah, right. Nevertheless, I gave the move some thought. I really wanted to jump out there and agree to what he was throwing my way, but I needed more time to think about it. What he was talking about was some serious shit. Not only could I get popped and go to prison forever, but I had to think about other risks as well. For example, what would happen if I didn't get the coke where it was supposed to go? What if somebody was to rob me and kill me for the coke? I really had to think about all that could come with making moves for Twin.

"I'm feelin' what you talkin' about, but I need more time to think it over before I jump out there and tell you I can do it."

He nodded. With a smile he said, "I feel you. I respect that. Just think about it and let me know what you come up with."

"Cool. I'll get back at you and let you know something in a couple of days."

"No problem." He handed me the shopping bag with the bricks in it.

I took the money out of my backpack and sat it on the coffee table. All $85,000 of it.

Twin looked at the money and said, "Our business is done for now. Get back with me soon. Let me know what you want to do."

"I will." I put the bricks in my backpack and hit the road.

* * *

Back home, inside my apartment, I spoke to Jay about the proposition Twin threw my way. I was giving it a lot of thought. Jay told me that I should make the move. He said that Twin was a real dude and that it was always good to have niggaz like Twin in your corner if you were trying to make some real money.

Sitting on the sofa in my living room, Jay said, "That's a sweet move, for real-for real. You can't beat that $5,000 every trip. Shit, in four trips, you sittin' on twenty Gs, just like that. You don't have to do it for no long time. Just get down for a second, and you gon' have a nice little piece of change put up before the summer is over. I'm tryin' to tell you some good shit, baby girl."

I nodded. "I might have to make that move. I'm gon' think about it a little more, though."

"Cool. It's your call. I'm wit' whatever you wanna do."

I thought about the money I could make fucking with Twin. The money was calling me. With the right amount of paper, I was sure I could get my mother out of prison, or at least get her a good lawyer and get her time cut down some. That would mean the world to me. Aside from that, I could also afford my own spot somewhere. After a little more thought, I decided to take it slow. I was already taking enough risks. I didn't need to add anything else to what I was doing at the time.

I looked at Jay and said, "I'm gon' lay on that move with Twin right now. I got my hands full."

Jay said, "Cool, I feel you. Like I said, that's your call." He stood up and began looking at text messages on his cell phone. He sent a quick text to someone and then said to me, "I gotta go take care of some shit real quick." He pulled out a knot of cash out of his pocket and handed it to me. "That's another G right there. I need you to cook them other joints for me, cool?"

I nodded. "I got you."

"Troy gon' come by and grab them joints, cool?"

"Cool."

"Make sure he give you the money."

"Okay," I said.

Jay left.

I rolled myself a J and got in the tub for a second. When I was done, I went to work and broke out the Pyrex pot, baking soda, and a little ammonia. At the stove, I put my whip game down and turned five bricks of powder into seven and a half bricks of hard white like it was nothing. I let them air out for a hot second, wrapped them in plastic, and then set them on the dining room table. With all the risks I was taking, it was time to start looking out for self a little bit. I decided to hold two and a half bricks for myself. The way I saw it, if I could find a way to get rid of the coke that would be a strong $50,000 in my stash.

My cell phone rang as I was thinking about dollars. I grabbed the phone. It was my moms calling. I pressed 5 off the top and accepted the call.

"Niya," she said.

"What's up, Ma?"

"Not too much. I got that money you sent me. It was right on time. Thanks, baby. You always come through."

"That's what I'm here for. Anytime you need something, just ask, and I will find a way to do it."

"That's why I love you, girl."

My moms voice didn't sound right. Something was wrong with her. She sounded down or stressed out.

"Ma, you okay?"

"Yeah, I'm good. Just dealing with being in here. Anyway, let me ask you something, Niya."

"What's up, Ma?"

"What are you into out there?"

That caught me off guard. I didn't know what she was talking about. I was sure there was no way she could know what I was really doing as far as drugs and trips to New York.

"What you mean by that, Ma?"

"Niya, I been around for a long time. I have seen a lot of things, and I know when certain things are not adding up. You work in a book store, you struggling, you out there on your own. How can you afford to send me $250?"

I had to think fast. I knew where she was going with this. It's the same way she used to go at Jaz.

"Well … Jay paid the rent for me this month, so I had a few extra dollars. I thought you could use it, Ma."

"A few extra dollars, huh?" Sarcasm filled her voice.

I was so uncomfortable; I hated lying to my mother. However, I couldn't tell her what the real deal was.

"What are you getting' at, Ma?"

She sighed. "Like I said, I been around for a long time, Niya. It ain't too much I ain't seen in this world. I know how shit go, baby. Be very careful out there. Whatever you do, make sure you think it all the way through. I pray you don't get yourself caught up in no bad situation."

I didn't even respond. What could I say? My moms was no fool; she knew how things worked in the streets.

"You mixed up with Jay, ain't you?"

I couldn't keep lying to her. "In a way. I really don't want to talk about it on the phone, Ma, but yeah, I'm dealin' wit' him in a way. But nothing too serious."

My moms sighed with disappointment. I knew what she was thinking. She felt like I was going down the same road as my sister when she started getting caught up in the street life. But on the real, my situation was different in my eyes. In my eyes, I was doing what I had to do for a second, until I could get my situation in order. Once my situation was in order, I was going to leave the whole drug game alone and move on. I was doing what I had to do to survive.

"Niya, let me school you to somethin', somethin' you should already be hip to: Ain't nothing in this world free, baby. When I was in the life, I always shot down handouts. Shit that's offered for free is dangerous, unless you know where the person's kindness is comin' from for sure. I don't know what Jay is up to when he comes to you, but I'm sure his kindness comes with some kind of hidden expectations."

My mother's words hit me hard. She was making a lot of sense. Yet, on the other hand, the way I saw it at the time, Jay was my meal ticket for a minute. He was making sure I was okay. I was no fool either. I knew he was using me, but I was using him too. I was using him for connections. I was making sure that I was putting myself in a position to make a come-up, by any means.

"Just be smart, Niya. You have always been a thinker. Never play the fool, you hear me?"

"I hear you, Ma, loud and clear. I understand where you comin' from."

"Everything comes with a price, Niya. A price and a risk. Never forget that. We had it good when I was home doing my thing, but at the same time, the price for all of that is the reason I'm sitting in prison right now. So what I'm saying to you is this: Judge every move you make out there by the price you gon' have to pay for it in the end."

"I feel you, Ma."

"I'm going to leave it at that. We'll talk some more when I see you next time."

"Okay."

"On another tip, I got some legal mail yesterday. The courts denied my last motion for a new trial."

I sighed and shook my head. "So what's next, Ma? What else can you do to get out of there?"

She sighed. "I have to go to the law library and find somethin' else to file. That's all I can do. I spoke to my lawyer this morning, and he said he don't think it's too much else we can about this case here."

"I'ma' find you another lawyer, a good one!" I blurted.

"Niya, I told—"

"No, Ma, I got this. Let me do this. I got some things goin' on. If the lawyer you got ain't gettin' the job done—"

"No, Niya, I—"

"I'm gonna do it, Ma. I'm gonna find you a better lawyer. That's what I want to do. I need you out here with me."

My moms sighed. "You just like your father, Niya—he couldn't be told nothin' when he had his mind set on somethin'."

"I understand all that, Ma, but I gotta do what I gotta do. I hope you understand."

"Be careful, Niya. Please don't get yourself in trouble. Please do that for me."

Before I could say another word the phone hung up on me. I didn't even hear the click before it hung up because of how much I was talking. I sat there with the phone in my hand, just thinking about all my moms had said to me. But my mind was made up. I was going to get her out of prison, even if it was the last thing I did on earth.

I needed cash. I knew exactly how I was going to get it, too!

I grabbed Jay's five bricks, put them in the backpack, and set them in the back of my closet. I grabbed my two and a half bricks and put them in my Louis Vuitton bag.

My next move would be to find someone to take the coke off of my hands for a good price. I knew I had to keep my business low. I didn't even want Jay to know what I was about to do. I had to be careful about who I dealt with.

Seconds later, there was a knock at my front door.

It had to be Troy coming to pick up the coke that Jay was talking about.

I went to the door and looked through the peephole. My heart skipped a beat. Fear ran through my body. Slowly, I backed away from the door wondering what I should do next. I took a deep breath and tried to get my thoughts together.

The police were at my door.

Trappin' Ain't Dead

I was looking into the eyes of the same homicide detective who had questioned me about Tyriq's murder. The detective was at my door. What the fuck could he want? I had nothing to say to him, nothing at all. Hear no evil, see no evil, say no names—that's how I was raised. That was the code, and I lived by that, no questions asked.

I refused to open the door.

The detective knocked again. Harder this time. He was making it clear that he wasn't going to leave.

I kept quiet, wanting him to think no one was home. I hoped that would make him leave. I walked away from the door, softly, not wanting him to hear a sound inside the apartment. I sat on the sofa, nervous as hell, praying he'd go away. I thought about the coke in my bedroom and began to sweat.

My phone buzzed. It was Face calling. I was going have to call him back later.

The detective knocked once more. Three hard pounds.

Damn! His hot ass was pressed like shit, for real. I wasn't opening the door. He would have to do better than that. I continued to sit there like I wasn't home.

A few minutes later, I heard footsteps going down the hall. I hoped the detective was going the fuck on about his business.

I eased into my bedroom and called Face back. He answered the phone like he was pleased to hear from me.

"What's up, girl?"

"Ain't too much," I said. The homicide detective's visit still had me a little nervous. For all I knew, he could still be outside in his car waiting on me to show my face in public.

"I got a few dollars to spend. You feel like goin' out somewhere? Maybe another movie and then chill over my joint?"

I smiled. "Back to your joint, huh?"

He laughed. "I ain't mean it like that, but you can take it like that if you want to. I don't have nothin' against that there any day of the week. But on the real, I just wanna spend some time with you. You been on my mind real heavy these past few days."

That made me blush. "You been on my mind too. A lot."

"So what's good, Niya? You tryin' to spend some time wit' a nigga or what? I'm missin' you."

"Yeah, we can hook up. Let me take care of a few things first. I'ma' call you back when I'm done. Cool?"

"That's a bet, sexy. Hit me soon as you done."

"I got you."

When I got off the phone with Face, I smiled and shook my head. I was feeling him, for real. It was just something about him that kept me interested. He wasn't like other dudes his age. He had things on his mind. He had goals and ambition, shit I respected in a nigga.

While I was thinking about Face, there was another knock at my door. I couldn't believe the detective was back. He had to be real pressed to come back. I headed for the front door slowly to see who it was. I looked through the peephole and saw Troy. Swiftly, I let him in and looked up and down the hall real quick to make sure the detective wasn't out there watching my apartment. When I saw no detective in sight, I shut the door.

Troy looked at me like I was crazy. "What's up with you, Niya? You lunchin' off the water or somethin'?"

I laughed at his remark. He knew damn well I didn't fuck around with P.C.P.

"Whatever, boy. You know I don't fuck with no dippers. The feds was just at my door." I told him what just went down.

"Oh yeah?" He looked like that information made him nervous. "What he want you for, that shit about Tyriq?"

"I don't know, but I ain't got no time to be talkin' to no feds. I don't even want nobody to see them peoples at my door, feel me? I don't know what made him think I was gon' open my door for his cracker ass. I already told him before that I don't know shit so don't ask me a damn thing. I ain't gon' help them peoples build a case against nobody. I don't know shit about Tyriq or whoever the fuck smoked his ass."

Troy rubbed his chin like he was in deep thought. He then shook his head and said, "You might need to talk to the detective just to get him off your ass. Or get a lawyer or somethin' to step to them peoples."

I thought about what he said, but I didn't want to talk to the police again about some murder shit that I ain't have shit to do with.

"I feel you, but I ain't got no rap for them peoples," I said with a little attitude.

"I understand where you comin', from but if the joker keep pressin' you, you gon' have to holla at him sooner or later. Just tell him the same thing over and over. He'll get fed up and leave you alone."

I sighed. "I'll think about it, but if he keep pressin' me, I'ma just get a lawyer."

Troy nodded. "That might be the move there."

"You know a good lawyer I can holla at?"

"Yeah, I know a few good lawyers, but you don't want to drop no serious paper on no lawyer for no shit like that."

"It ain't just for that shit. I'm tryin' to get my mother a new lawyer anyways."

"Oh, I feel you. She still fightin' that coke charge?"

"Yeah," I nodded.

"I know a good lawyer. The nigga's a monster wit' them drug cases and appeals cases. His name John Sherman. He got my man's murder conviction overturned last year. It's the same lawyer Jay had on his gun beef."

I was interested. "How much a lawyer like that gon' run me?"

"My man gave him twenty-five thousand, but his case was real fucked up; he had all kinds of witnesses against him. In the end, the nigga John found a lot of fucked-up shit in the transcripts that got the judge to overturn the case and give my man a new trial. The government ain't want to spend no more money on a new trial, so they didn't fight the shit. They let him walk just like that. So if it's anything that can be done for your mother's case, he will find it and fight the issues like shit. Check him out."

"I need his number."

"I'ma text it to you right now." Troy pulled out his phone and texted me the number.

"I'm gon' give him a call and see what's good. I need to get her out of there. No bullshit." My phone chimed; it was the lawyer's number. "I got it. I'm lockin' it in right now. Thanks, Troy."

Ain't no thing. You family, Niya."

He looked around the apartment as he put his phone back in his pocket. His eyes lingered on the $3,000 laying on the coffee table. I was so focused on the coke that I forgot to put my money up. I really didn't want him to see that kind of money just laying around my apartment. I didn't need him in my business like that, but there was nothing I could do about it now.

Troy looked at me and said, "I ain't tryin' to be all up in your business, but I think you startin' to move a little fast wit' the shit you doin', Niya."

I didn't know what the fuck that was supposed to mean. "What you mean by that?"

"Come on, Niya. I ain't no fool. I'm hip to what you doin'. I be wit' Jay every day."

I caught an attitude and said, "I know what I'm doin'. I don't need or want a father, Troy."

He sighed and slightly shook his head. "It ain't like that, Niya. I just think you movin' too fast in a game that you don't know much about. The streets are mean."

"You don't think I know that, Troy?"

"I know you know what goes on out here. You ain't green, but shit is on a whole different level when you fuck around in the drug game. This shit is serious. Look at your mother's situation. Shit, on the real, Jay dead wrong for gettin' you mixed up in this shit. I told him I don't like it. He know better. He know your mother would be fucked up at him if she knew what you was doin'. Even Jaz wouldn't go for no shit like that either."

"Troy, I'm grown. I don't have to ask nobody for permission to do what I want to do. My mother ain't here and Jaz ain't here either! I'm doin' what I gotta do. So if you ain't gon' pay my bills and get my mother a lawyer, then it really ain't too much you can say to me, is there?"

Troy shook his head and sighed with frustration.

It was all good that he cared enough about me to say something, but it would be better for him to stay the fuck out of my business. I had shit to do and I planned to do whatever it took for me to handle my business. It was no way around that.

"I feel exactly where you comin' from. At the same time I got a lot of love for you. I got a lot of love and respect for your mother as well. I wouldn't even jump out there and say shit if I didn't care. I just don't want to see you get caught up in this shit. It's a dirty game, Niya. You just don't know. I'm tryin' to tell you."

I really wasn't used to Troy coming at me in such a way. I was used to him always joking with me or trying to get between my legs. Nevertheless, I sighed and said, "Look, Troy, I understand where you comin' from, and I appreciate the fact that you care. I really do. I respect that, but I'm doin' what I gotta do. It ain't a whole lot to it. Simple as that."

The look on his face made it clear that he got my point. He shrugged and said, "Okay, just be careful, Niya." He took a deep breath, rubbed his chin, and added, "You got them joints for me?"

"Yeah, I got that for you. You got the money?"

Troy looked at me like I was crazy. "The money? I'ma' give Jay the money after I take care of a few things. You know how me and slim go."

I shook my head no and said, "Jay told me to make sure I got the paper from you." I shrugged like it was out of my hands. "That's what he said. You can call him and ask him yourself."

Troy had a look of disbelief on his face. "Niya, you serious?"

"That's what Jay said."

"Cool." I could tell Troy was pissed off by the way he snatched his cell phone out of the holster on the side of his belt. He called Jay. "Ay, Jay, you told Niya I gotta give her the paper up front?"

I listened to the quick conversation. Sure enough, Jay stood on what he had said to me. I don't know why, but something was wrong between them. Troy ended the call with a pissed-off look on his face. He looked at me and said, "I gotta go get the paper. I'll be right back." He left.

Fifteen minutes later, Troy was knocking on the door again. I let him in. This time he had a brown paper bag with him. He handed me the paper bag and said, "That's for Jay. It's all there."

I grabbed the bag and looked inside. "How much is this?"

"Fifty thousand."

"Cool, I'll be right back." I took the money and went to get the coke for him. I came back in the living room with the bricks in a Gucci shopping bag. "Here you go."

"Cool." He took the bag and left like he had a beef with me for not giving him the bricks without getting the money. I shook my head. It wasn't my fault that Jay wanted his money up front.

I pushed all of that out of my mind and sat on the sofa. My mother's situation was more important than anything else. That's where my mind went. I pulled out my phone and called the lawyer Troy hipped me to. He didn't answer, so I left a message. I decided to take a trip downtown to his office as soon as possible. It was a must that I find a lawyer, all bullshit aside.

Another knock on my door grabbed my attention. *Who the fuck is it this time?* I got up and went to see who was at my door. It was my girl Lisa. I let her in, looked her up and down, and said, "Damn, girl, you look good."

Lisa smiled. "Thanks, Niya."

Lisa had on a white linen outfit by Roberto Cavalli and some sexy-ass heels to match. Her hair and nails were done perfectly. I wasn't surprised. She took pride in staying fly at all times. It was her thing.

"Where the hell you goin'?"

Lisa put her hands on her hips and said, "Damn, why a bitch gotta be goin' somewhere to look good?"

I laughed. "My bad, diva. Excuse me."

Lisa sat on the sofa and said, "I'm 'bout to go meet my baby. We goin' to Philly to holla at his cousin. I guess I'll hit the mall while we up there. You know me, bitch. Prada, Gucci, Marc Jacobs—I gotta have it all. No question about it."

I shook my head and smiled. "You spend all your paper in the mall, don't you?"

"Please! When I'm wit' my baby, it ain't my money I'm spending, it's his."

I gave her five and laughed. "I know that's right, bitch! Work your shit. I ain't mad at you."

"It ain't trickin' if you got it!" she said.

We both died laughing.

Still laughing, I said, "Lisa, bitch, you crazy."

"Come on, Niya, I'ma boss bitch, a diva. I'm supposed to be treated like royalty, feel me?"

"Yeah, I feel you on that."

I looked at my money while we were talking. I'd forgotten to put it up, again. *Damn!* It was still on the coffee table. I really needed to put the money up.

"Hold on for a second. Let me put this paper up."

"I see you making moves."

I smiled as I picked up the money. "Like you be sayin': A bitch gotta eat."

She laughed. "I know that's right."

I took the money in the bedroom and went back in the living room.

Lisa said, "You been makin' some moves, huh?"

"Yeah, a little bit." I needed Lisa for what I was trying to do so I was cool with the conversation. She was always about paper and knew how to get it on all levels. She'd been that way for as long as I could remember.

"What you got goin' on, Niya?"

I sat on the sofa. "Look, we gotta keep this shit between me and you, feel me?"

"You know you don't even have to say that when it comes to me and you. What's good, though?"

"Jaz used to cook coke for a few dudes and tax 'em a G every time she whipped the shit for them. So in so many words, I'm telling you I got the whip game down. I know a few dudes, so I figured I could use the cash. So anyway, I'm putting a little coke to the side to sell."

Lisa nodded. "Oh, yeah, that's what's up. You gotta get the change. If it ain't about paper, then its bullshit. So you get a G for every joint you cook? That's sweet. So what you gon' do, be on the block, pumpin'?"

I laughed. "Fuck no. Cut the bullshit out. On a serious tip, I want to off the shit in chunks. I know you know some niggaz that will grab the shit from me, right?"

"Yeah, that ain't no thing."

"Cool, 'cause I really don't want niggaz around here in my business. Feel me?"

"Yeah, no doubt. That's how it's supposed to be done. I know a few dudes that fuck around wit' that white. I can check and let you know what's good. I would holla at my uncle, but he said they givin' out thirty years for that crack—all he fuck wit' is pills and weed now. But let me holla at Dee and them and see what my baby say. He got a lot of niggaz around First and Kennedy.

"Cool, that's what I'm talkin' about. I'll make sure it's somethin' in it for you too. You know how we go."

"Yeah, I feel you, that's all good. But on another tip, you know who you should really holla at."

"Terri?"

"Exactly," Lisa said with a nod.

We laughed and gave each other five. Terri knew everybody's business.

"You know that girl keep her ear to the streets. She always knows what's goin' on."

"Yeah, I know, I'ma holla at her today."

"How much coke you tryin' to sell?"

"Right now, I got two and a half bricks."

"Damn, you ain't bullshittin'."

"Fuck no, I ain't playin'. I'm tryin' to get some paper. I know dudes that's payin' twenty-eight thousand for bricks right now. Some payin' thirty-plus. I can grab me some quick change if all works out for me."

"Sounds like a plan to me. Shit, money makes the world go 'round. A bitch gotta eat. Let me check on a few things. I'm sure Dee will know somethin' good."

"That's what I'm talkin' 'bout. I knew you would come through for me," I said with a smile.

My cell phone rang. I looked at the screen and said, "Speak of the devil."

Lisa laughed. "Who is that, Terri?"

"You know it."

I answered the phone.

* * *

A little while later, I was sitting on the sofa with Terri talking about what I was trying to do. Lisa had left to go hook up with her boyfriend. Terri was down with the move. She was always down for whatever. I loved that about her. She knew three niggaz who would take the coke off my hands. That's what I was talking about. She made a phone call to one of her friends and set the shit in motion, just like that.

When she ended the phone call, she looked at me and said, "Niya, get one of them joints you got. My nigga Ray got the paper right now. We can go grab that right now."

"How much paper he got right now?" I asked.

"He got twenty-five. That's cool, right?"

"No doubt, that's cool. I can live wit' that," I said as I went to get a brick of coke from the bedroom. I returned to the living room with the coke in a black Prada handbag. "Your friend don't need to know where this shit came from, cool?"

Terri waved me off and said, "Don't trip off that, Niya. I'll tell 'em I got the shit from my cousin."

I smiled and shook my head. "You too much, girl."

"Believe that." She stood up. "Come on, let's go get this paper, Niya."

I grabbed the keys to the Range, and we left the apartment.

* * *

It was just getting dark outside when we pulled up on Rock Creek Church Road. A few dudes were standing in a pack in the middle of the block; they all looked like they were in their late teens and early 20s. I pulled into a parking space at the end of the block and cut off the truck. Terri pulled out her cell phone and made a call to a dude named Ray. She told him we were in the Range Rover at the end of the block. She ended the call, looked at me, and said, "Here he come."

I looked in the rearview mirror and saw a brown-skin dude with long dreads coming our way. It had to be Ray. I'd seen him somewhere before, but I couldn't put my finger on where. "Your boy look like Lil Wayne wit' the dreads and tats and shit," I said.

"Girl, all these niggaz look like Lil Wayne nowadays."

We both laughed like shit.

Terri said, "Let me get that." She grabbed the Prada bag off my lap and held it in her hand. She was going to handle everything with Ray for me. In my mind, that's the way it needed to be. Besides, she was the one who knew the nigga. As far as I was concerned, the less Ray knew about me the better.

"Cool," Ray said as he jumped in the back of the truck. He shut the door and looked at me. Cutting his eyes at Terri, he said, "Ay, Terri, who's your friend?"

"That's my girl. She cool. Don't worry about her."

Ray raised his eyebrows and said, "Okay, well, where the yay at?"

"I got it right here." Terri handed him the Prada bag.

He looked inside.

Terri said, "Where the paper at?"

Ray smiled and said, "Where you get this shit from, Terri?"

Terri smiled. "All you need to know is that the shit is good. It's what it's supposed to be, boo."

"Cool, you right. I trust you."

"Cool." Terri held out her hand. "Where the paper?"

Ray said, "Why don't we pull into the alley."

I didn't like that. I began to have thoughts of us getting robbed in the alley. However, I pushed those thoughts out of my head. Terri wouldn't get us caught up like that. I tried to make myself feel comfortable.

Terri looked at me and said, "Go 'head and pull into the alley. We good."

"Okay." I started the truck up and pulled into the alley, watching Ray in my rearview the whole time.

When we got in the alley, Ray said, "Pull up behind that black Bronco."

I did just that and put the truck in park. For some reason, I didn't want to turn the joint off.

Ray got out and went inside the Bronco. He returned with a brown paper bag and handed it to Terri through the window. "It's all there. You know I'm good, sexy."

"I believe you," Terri said as she looked inside the paper bag.

Ray leaned inside the window and said, "If you run across some more of this shit, make sure you holla at a nigga."

"You know I will." Ray kissed Terri on the cheek, then walked down the alley with the coke.

It was a wrap. Just like that, we'd made $25,000. Inside, I was siced. I looked at Terri and smiled. She'd really come through for me.

She handed me the paper bag and said, "It's simple as that. You good now."

"Thank you, Terri," I said as I pulled off.

"I'm sure all the money is there, but we can count it when we get back to your apartment."

"Okay," I said. It felt good to make that much cash at one time, in seconds. If shit was to keep going like that, I would have a new lawyer for my mother in no time. All my worries would be behind me.

At least that's what I thought.

* * *

Me and Terri counted the money when we got back to my apartment. It was straight. Twenty-five thousand on the nose. It was a quick come-up. I knew Terri could make it happen for me. Nevertheless, I was still impressed with the fact that she got right on top of the situation for me.

Terri looked at me and said, "So you can put a whole brick to the side whenever you cook for a nigga?"

"Depends on how good the coke is. The nigga that got me to cook that last shit had some serious shit, grade A, so I was able to put my game on it and put something to the side. Plus it depends on how much I'm cooking too. The thing is for me to stretch the coke without a nigga knowin' I stretched the coke. Feel me?"

"Okay, I see what you sayin'."

"I gotta look out for me, ain't no question."

"One thing I can say about you and your sister is you two always knew how to make ends meet."

"I get it from my momma," I joked.

Terri laughed. "Money makes the world go 'round."

"No bullshit." I gave her five. "I hear that."

"Okay!" she nodded.

I grabbed two stacks off the coffee table and handed them to Terri. I had to hit her off with something. It was only right. I believed in playing fair as much as I could.

"This is for me?" Terri asked, smiling.

"Yeah, good lookin' out. You came through for me and I respect that, one hundred. I really need this paper. I'm tryin' to get my moms outta prison. She needs a lawyer bad, and I'm all she has. I gotta come through for her."

"That's what's up, Niya. That's some real shit there."

"It's my mother. I gotta do all I can to help her. That's how she raised me."

"I feel you. Here," she said, offering me the money back. "I can't take your money. I understand what you're tryin' to do."

"No, Terri, keep the money. Do that for me. I appreciate what you did for me."

"Okay. Thanks, Niya."

"It's all good. You my girl. It ain't nothin' to it. Besides, I'm gon' need your help again real soon."

Terri nodded. "I got you. Don't even trip. Just call me when you need to make a move."

"Okay."

"Ay, Niya, can you do me a favor though?"

"Yeah. What's up?"

"Show me how you cook that coke up and stretch it. I know a few dudes that be buying that shit. I may be able to make me a few dollars on the side too. Feel me?"

I thought about what she was asking of me for a second. I had never shown anyone how to whip coke; my sister always told me to keep that to myself. Jaz used to say that if a motherfucker didn't know how to go to work at the stove, then they were just late. That was the way she schooled me. But Terri was my girl. I decided that I would give her the game.

"Yeah, I got you. Next time I make a move I'ma put you down. Okay?"

"That's what I'm talkin' about. You that bitch, Niya."

We both laughed.

<u>Secrets Never Die</u>

"I'm out front," I said to Face as I sat behind the wheel of the Range on 14th Street, holding my cell phone to my ear.

"I'm on my way out, sexy," Face said.

I smiled as I put my phone inside my Louis Vuitton bag. I was really feeling Face. It was just something about him. I couldn't believe I was picking a nigga up to go chill; I was used to niggaz picking me up. But it was all good.

Seconds later, Face came out and jumped in the truck, all smiles. He looked happy to see me. Armani cologne filled the inside of the truck. I knew that smell well, and I loved it on Face.

"Damn, you smell good."

I pulled into traffic.

"Just got out of the shower. Got all fresh for you, you know?" he winked.

I laughed. "You too much, boy."

Face was looking good. He had on a black and red Polo shirt, blue jean shorts, and a pair of black Jordans. His dreads were pulled back into a ponytail.

"So where we goin'?" I asked.

"I was thinkin' we could hit Georgetown, you know, just chill for a little while."

"Sounds good to me." I headed toward Georgetown, which wasn't far from our part of town.

As we cruised through traffic, Face said, "You know what, Niya?"

"What's that?"

"One day I'm gon' be pickin' you up in my own shit. I'm gon' get me somethin' real nice, like a Benz or somethin'. I'm gon' get on my feet and treat you real good, you feel me?"

I smiled. "Is that right?"

"On everything I love." Face rubbed my face with the back of his hand. "I'm feelin' you, Niya. You special."

I felt like a little girl. I was all smiles. Something about being around Face made me feel at ease, comfortable.

"I got somethin' for you, somethin' special." Face went in his pocket and pulled out a little velvet box.

My eyebrows went up. I said, "What's that, Face?" It couldn't be what I thought it was. He had me feeling special.

"Check this out, Niya." Face opened the box and pulled out a beautiful white gold necklace with diamonds in it. "You like it?"

With a huge smile on my face, I said, "It's beautiful, Face. I love it." I stopped at a red light and let him put the necklace around my neck.

"It looks good on you, Niya. I want you to think of me every time you lay eyes on this joint, okay?"

"Okay, I can do that." The light turned green and I headed across 16th Street into Rock Creek Park. "When did you get this for me?"

"I went out and got it for you earlier today. I was thinkin' about you . Thought you would like it."

"You were right. I love it, boo. You scored, big time."

Face smiled. I could tell that it made him feel good to make me smile. He was really my kind of nigga.

"It's just something small. Like I said, I was just thinkin' about you. I got a few dollars in advance from South Side. I thought I'd get you something real nice— you and my mother."

"Ain't that sweet of you?" I joked.

We both laughed.

"You got jokes, don't you? You funny as shit, Niya."

"Whatever, Face," I shrugged, smiling.

Face leaned over and kissed me on the lips real soft-like. "I'm really feelin' you. That's on everything. I can't get you off my mind."

"Cut it out, boy."

"For real. I mean it. I think about you all the time."

I was flattered. "I feel you, Face. I think about you all the time too."

The vibe between us was good.

"That's what's up."

I cut my eyes at him real quick and added, "You not pussy whipped, are you?"

Face laughed. "I know you ain't talkin' shit. The way you was moanin' and cummin' when we was doin' the damn thing, I thought I had you whipped."

It was my turn to laugh. "Nigga, please. You know what's up, for real."

"Let's see what's good tonight after we get back."

The thought of being with him made me tingle.

"You ain't said nothin' but a word, boo. We gon' see what's good."

"Bet."

His cell phone went off, cutting into our conversation. He pulled the phone out and checked to see who was calling. He let the call go to voice mail. His facial expression changed; he looked irritated.

"You okay, Face?"

He sighed, shook his head and said, "Ain't nothin'."

"Shit, I can't tell. You look like somebody pissed you off. Tell me somethin'."

Face sighed. I could tell he didn't want to talk about whatever was bothering him.

"I don't even feel like talkin' about that shit. I'm tryin' to chill wit' you."

"I understand, but I can tell somethin' is on your mind. You can talk to me."

Face took a deep breath and looked into my eyes as he rubbed his chin. "Check this out, and don't take it the wrong way, okay?"

I nodded in agreement.

"I used to fuck wit' this broad a while back, but I had to cut her off. She was too loose for me, you dig what I'm sayin'? Anyway, all of a sudden now she callin' my phone talkin' 'bout I got a son by her and shit. The whole time she was pregnant I ain't know shit about it. I don't believe shit that come out of her mouth. I think she just tryin' to find a nigga to put the baby on."

I sighed. I really wasn't in the mood for no bullshit. I didn't have time for that kind of shit in my life. I had enough to deal with.

"The baby ain't mine, Niya."

"Niggaz always say that." For some reason, I said that with a little attitude. "How you know for sure the baby ain't yours?"

Face sighed. He rubbed his chin. "That's why I didn't really want to talk about this shit. I had a feelin' you was gon' look at it like that."

"I'm just sayin' … how you know the baby ain't yours? You had to fuck the bitch, right or wrong?" I raised my voice a little bit. I could tell Face didn't like that.

He raised his voice. "Yeah, I fucked her, but I used a rubber every time!" Face took a deep breath and lowered his voice. "Niya, look, we ain't even gotta go through this here. That's on everything."

I sucked my teeth and rolled my eyes.

Face shook his head and said, "My mother told me to get a blood test to put an end to this shit, so that's what I'm gon' do now. Simple as that. Feel me?"

I thought about what he was saying for a second, and I couldn't figure out why I was so heated. Truth be told, Face wasn't my man. He and I were getting close, but at the end of the day, he still wasn't my man. Nevertheless, I still wanted him all to myself.

"You should get a blood test. That will dead the whole situation and bring the truth to light. That'll seal the deal."

"Will that make you feel better?"

I gave him a mean look. "You tryin' to be funny, Face?"

He laughed. "Nah, I ain't trying to be funny. But you just got real heated about the shit I told you, like I crossed you or somethin'."

"I been through a lot, Face. I don't want my feelings and shit caught up wit' you if you got baby momma drama. I really ain't wit' all that shit. I know how I get. I will snap."

Face nodded. "I feel you on that. Don't even trip. The shit ain't nothin'. I put that on my mother."

"Okay, I'm gon' trust you on this. Don't make me out to be the fool."

"Never that. Don't even trip."

A short while later, we found a parking space. As always, Georgetown was busy and full of life. People were everywhere, going in and out of stores and restaurants. White couples were out walking their dogs. Young blacks were out and about as well, shopping and looking good. I cut the truck off and was ready to chill for a little while. I needed the chill time.

Face grabbed my hand softly and said, "So we cool, right? It's all good?"

I playfully gave him an evil look and said, "Yeah, we good for now, but don't make me hurt you."

He laughed.

I laughed a little as well, but I was dead serious at the same time. I wasn't into getting caught up in someone else's bullshit — if I could help it.

* * *

We had a good time. We went to see the movie "Taken." I enjoyed it. Face had his arm around me the whole time. Every now and then he would kiss my neck or lick and suck on my ear. All that extra shit had me thinking about some other things. I was looking forward to spending some time alone with him when we got back to our part of town.

As we exited the movies, with a crowd of people behind us, Face put his arm around me again. I was feeling like his "girl." I could tell he was really feeling me. He leaned closer to my ear and whispered, "Where we goin' now? Back to your place?"

"Back to my place don't sound bad at all." I smiled, feeling sexy as shit. I wanted Face to myself, all night long. I was in the mood for it.

The streets of Georgetown were still busy and crowded. Face and I darted through traffic and crossed the street. We were laughing and joking all the way, having a good time. I was in a comfort zone with Face.

Face said, "You wanna' get something to eat real quick, boo?"

"Yeah, we can do that," I said as I pulled the keys to the Range from my pocket. "Let's just grab some Chinese food and keep it movin'."

Face smiled. "I'm all for that. Let's make it happen. I'm hungry as shit!"

I shook my head, smiling, as I unlocked the door on the driver's side.

"Face! Ay, Face! I know you see me! You gon' act like you don't see me?!" someone shouted. "I know you hear me callin' your ass."

I turned my attention to the sidewalk and saw three hood-rat bitches approaching Face. The light-skin one in the middle was the one shouting his name like she had lost her damn mind.

Light-skin shouted again, "Nigga, I know you hear me! I been callin' your phone over and over again, and you act like you can't pick up. You duckin' me now, huh? That's how we goin'? When the fuck did we get there?"

Face looked embarrassed and pissed off at the same time. He had a murderous, look on his face like he was about to go off on the bitch.

The bitch was making a scene, had people looking in our direction like we were on some dumb-ass reality show. I hated bitches who made scenes about dumb shit. I tried my best to stay from all the bullshit.

Frustration covered his face like a mask. He glared at the bitch and hissed, "Look, Dena, don't start the bullshit! I ain't in the mood for it, I'm tellin' you! You makin' a fuckin' scene! Cut it out!"

I rushed around the truck and posted up right beside Face with my game face on. I was ready to work. I glared at the light-skin bitch and her partners. The bitches returned the favor, like they were ready to put in some work. I didn't give a fuck. I didn't need to run in a pack to hold my own. I was waiting for one of them to say some slick shit to me. If one of them even looked at me the wrong way, I was gonna to take shit to a whole 'nother level .

Dena, the loud-mouth, light-skin bitch, put her hands on her hips and looked me up and down with disdain. I gritted right back on her ass. She looked at Face and said, "Face, who the fuck is this, you new girlfriend or somethin'?"

Tension was thick and building by the second.

Face put his arm around me and said, "Dena, it's none of your business who my girl is or who I'm out with, for that matter. You need to check yourself and keep it movin'."

I couldn't help it. I cut in and said, "I'm his girl! Now what?!" I said that with nothing but venom in my voice.

Face tried to tell me to let him handle the situation, but I really wasn't trying to hear that shit. The bitch had pissed me off. It was nothing Face could tell me.

Dena's friend, Hood Rat #2, jumped out there and said, "Ain't nobody talkin' to you, bitch!" She rolled her eyes and snaked her neck as she spoke, thinking she was really saying something slick.

That was all I needed. I stepped forward. Face tried to grab me, but I snatched away. Getting in the bitch's face, I said, "Bitch, I will put my foot in your funky ass! Try me!"

"Whatever," she said.

"Whatever my ass!"

Face grabbed me again. "Calm down, Niya!"

"Fuck that!" I tried to snatch away again, but he wouldn't let me go this time.

The bitches looked like they were trying to find the heart to make a move on me. Hood Rat #3 slid her hand inside her fake-ass Prada bag like she had a weapon.

Dena smiled wickedly, looking at Face, and said, "Face, you better get your little girlfriend before she get fucked up out here."

Face said, "Ain't nothin' gon' happen to her. You need to take your little crew and keep steppin'. That baby ain't mine. We gon' get a blood test, and that's gon' be the end of this shit."

Dena shouted, "You can get all the blood work you want, muthafucka. It's your baby! Ain't nothin' gon' change that!"

"Let me go, Face!" I shouted. I wanted to beat the shit out of all three of those bitches. I snatched away from Face and charged Hood Rat #2. I punched her right in the mouth and staggered her ass. She tried to come back with a punch of her own, but I popped her ass two more times real quick. She threw a wild-ass punch and caught me in the eye, making me see stars for a second. We traded punches as we grabbed each other's hair. We fought like we had been enemies all our lives. Dena and Hood Rat #3 were yelling and cursing, talking a bunch of shit as Face tried to break us up. I felt somebody grab my hair and yank me backwards. That didn't stop me; I was still going off like a caged panther.

"Get the fuck off her, bitch!" Face shouted. He yanked Dena off me and slung her to the ground like a rag doll.

I was dead on Hood Rat # 2's ass. I had a handful of her hair as I landed punch after punch right in her face. We both hit the ground as people began to gather around the drama. We were making a real ghetto scene right in the middle of Georgetown. With a good grip on her weave, I slammed my fist right into her face again and busted her nose. I could see the blood begin to flow. We wrestled around for a second, but I managed to get on top of her and commenced punishing her ass like she stole something. I didn't even feel the other punches and kicks coming from the other bitch. Hood Rat # 2 kept throwing wild punches. Some of them hit me in the face, but that didn't stop me. I was too pissed off to feel anything. I was in a zone. As far as I was concerned, the bitch was going to the hospital for a few days.

Meanwhile, Dena and Hood Rat #3 were trying to go at Face. Dena had gotten off the ground and rushed Face, swinging and yelling, "I hate you, muthafucka!" Face shoved her to the ground again. Hood Rat # 3 pulled a knife and tried to stab Face. He danced out of the way and twisted her arm. She screamed in pain. He took the knife from her with ease and threw it in the street.

"Hey! Hey!" a voice shouted from somewhere close by. Two D.C. cops were making their way through the small crowd that had gathered to watch this bullshit. People were looking at us like we were crazy. We had turned Georgetown into the hood.

One of the cops snatched me off Hood Rat # 2 and slung me against the wall. I was still going off. The cop shouted, "Calm down! Calm down before you end up in jail!"

Two more cops appeared. Then a cop car showed up with its sirens blaring and lights flashing. It was like a scene from "Cops."

In no time, the cops had all of us, except Hood Rat #2, against the wall of some store that sold leather coats. Hood Rat # 2 was out of it; she couldn't remember what day of the week it was. I had beat the shit out of her ass and left her battered and bruised like she'd run into the L.A.P.D. in the 90s on a dark highway. I didn't feel bad at all. Fuck her. She should have stayed in her fucking place. One of the cops helped Hood Rat # 2 to her feet and sat her on the curb to wait for the paramedics.

There was no doubt in my mind we were all on our way to the D.C. Jail.

* * *

Hood Rat # 2 didn't press charges against me. In fact, nobody pressed charges. Everybody got arrested for disorderly conduct. That was a blessing, for real. I didn't need a real charge. Hood Rat # 2 went to the hospital, as planned. Fuck her! I could deal with a punk-ass disorderly conduct beef for beating her ass. It was nothing. But there was something more waiting for me at the police station: A homicide detective wanted to question me. Homicide had put a warrant on me, and I didn't even know it.

"Why they want to talk to me down homicide?" I asked a lady cop, though I was pretty sure I already knew the answer.

Chewing her gum as she did my paperwork, she said, "You know something about a murder?"

That was enough to make me shut my damn mouth. "Nah, I don't know shit about no murder."

She looked at me sideways and said, "Somebody thinks otherwise, young lady."

I shrugged my shoulders and said nothing else.

* * *

Forty-five minutes later, I was sitting in a tiny interrogation room, feeling a little nervous. I was resting my head on the wooden table, waiting for the detective to come in and run some psychological bullshit on me. I really didn't know what to expect. All I knew for sure was that I had nothing to tell him about any murder. It wasn't my business. I wasn't in the mood to play any games. I just wanted to get the shit over with. The more I thought about the situation, the more I began to feel like I needed to get a lawyer—quick. I planned to demand a lawyer as soon as the detective came in so they would leave me the fuck alone.

Moments later, the door opened and in walked a brown-skin woman wearing blue jeans and a black T-shirt with red letters that spelled out: STOP THE KILLING. She was carrying a notepad in her hand and had a few folders, each stuffed with papers, under her arm. The woman looked 30-something. She sat across the table from me and smiled brightly.

"You're Niya, right?" the lady asked.

I sighed. "Come on, you know my name. Y'all got me down here wit' a warrant on me. You know my name. What do you want with me?"

The cop smiled. "You're right. Let's do it this way—my name is Detective Holmes. My partner,

Detective Phillips, interviewed you some time ago about the murder of a Tyriq Brown. You know what I'm talking about, right?"

I disregarded every word she said. "Are you charging me wit' a crime, 'cause if you are, I want a lawyer. If not, I wanna get the fuck outta here."

She shook her head. "I can charge you with obstruction of justice and being an accessory to murder if you want to play tough. You can spend a lot of time in prison for lying about what you know, Niya."

I smirked and shook my head. I couldn't believe she was coming at me with that bullshit. "I don't know a muthafuckin' thing. I already told your partner that. I wouldn't care if you sent me to Guantanamo Bay. I still wouldn't have shit to tell you. I don't know shit. Simple as that."

The door burst open. Detective Phillips stormed inside the room and shouted, "Stop lying, Niya!"

I jumped a little bit and looked at him like he was crazy. I guess he called himself trying to scare me.

He slammed his fist down on the table, got in my face and said, "We know you know who killed Tyriq Brown!"

I rolled my eyes at the clown. "All that damn yellin' and bangin' on shit ain't gon' make me tell you what I don't know."

Holmes stood up and said, "Let me speak to her alone, Phillips."

He glared at me like he wanted to choke the shit out of me. I could see it written all over his face. "Play tough if you want to, Niya. You'll be working in a prison kitchen for forty-five cents a day for ten years." He left the room and slammed the door behind him.

Holmes went inside one of her folders and pulled out some gruesome pictures of Tyriq, who was shot in the head at close range. She slid them across the table real slow-like so I'd get a good look. The shit made my stomach turn. Tyriq's brains were hanging out the side of his head, and his eyes were wide open. I had to look away. I couldn't take it.

"Not a pretty sight, is it?" she asked.

I didn't say a word. Seeing that picture made me think about my sister being shot in the head.

"I know all about the code of the streets, Niya, I really do. I know you don't want to talk to me, and I understand that. With that being said, I'm going to talk to you for a second. I'm going to share some things with you, and when I'm done talking, you can decide if you still want to protect Jay or not. I know for a fact that Jay killed Tyriq, and I know that you saw it. I just need to find a way to get you to tell me what you saw so I can put him away."

I looked surprised when she outright mentioned Jay's name. The other detective didn't mention Jay's name when he questioned me. Now they had more information. Somebody was telling!

"You look surprised, Niya. Didn't think we knew Jay did the killing? We know he did it. The streets talk. We knew he did it the night he did it, but we just couldn't prove it. We need an eyewitness, and you are that eyewitness. People are telling us you saw it and —"

"Why they ain't your eyewitness if they know so much?"

"They didn't see the shooter, but they saw you out there, and they all say you saw the shooter."

"They lyin'. I ain't see shit."

Holmes smiled and shook her head. She took a seat. "Let me tell you some more of what I know. I know Tyriq broke into Jay's apartment and stole $50,000. I know that's why he was murdered," she said, nodding as if she was letting me in on a secret. "I know how dangerous Jay is. I know you may fear what could happen if you tell me anything about him, but I can protect you. I won't let anything happen to you, Niya."

I laughed. "Yeah, right."

"Jay needs to be locked up, Niya. He needs to be taken off the streets before he kills someone else."

"And this all has what to do with me?"

She smiled. "Okay, let me share some more info with you." She pulled another picture from her folder and slid it across the table to me.

I snapped. My blood boiled. "What the fuck you showin' me that shit for?" I smacked the picture to the floor.

"Thought that would get your attention." She picked the picture up and put it back in her folder.

It was a picture of my sister, her bloody body slumped over behind the wheel of her Range Rover, shot to death. It was a murder scene picture. A murder scene picture I didn't need to see. That picture put a vision in my mind that would attack me in my sleep. I didn't need to see that shit.

"Let me share this with you as well: I also know that your sister was sleeping with Tyriq Brown."

I frowned. "Fuck you talkin' 'bout?!"

"Like I said, the streets talk. Come to find out your sister was seeing Tyriq on the side."

"Who told you some bullshit like that?!"

"People think your sister told Tyriq that fifty thousand was in Jay's apartment. She was seen with Tyriq the night he broke into Jay's apartment. Seems like your sister was playing both ends against the middle."

"I don't want to hear this shit!" I was steaming mad at this point.

She leaned back in her chair and said, "Guess who really killed your sister."

I glared at her with hate in my eyes. This bitch was trying to use my sister's death against me, trying to play games with my mind to make me tell on Jay.

"Jay killed your sister," she said.

"Stop lyin'!" I jumped to my feet. I didn't want to hear another word. I was getting emotional.

"Jay killed your sister. He killed your sister because he thought she set him up for Tyriq."

"Jaz would never do that! Jay would never hurt Jaz! You lyin'!"

"I have a witness that says Jay was the shooter the night your sister was murdered. We already have a warrant for his arrest."

I couldn't believe my ears.

"You still want to protect Jay?"

Slowly, I sat down. A million thoughts were going through my mind. I was questioning everything I knew about Jay. Deep inside, I couldn't believe that he would kill Jaz. I kept telling myself that the homicide detective was making it all up. I wanted to punch her in the damn face.

"I'm going to step out for a second and let you think about all that I just told you. I'll be back in a minute."

Leaving me alone with my thoughts, my doubts, and my anger.

My mind was all over the place. I kept telling myself the detective was lying. It was no way Jay killed Jaz and then turned around and made it seem like another nigga did it. I refused to believe that. It had to be bullshit.

Both detectives returned a short while later. Holmes took a seat across from me while Phillips leaned against the wall with a smug look on his face. He looked like he knew he had me where he wanted me. Holmes set a little recording device on the table and said, "Listen to this, Niya."

My heart skipped a beat, and my hands grew sweaty. I didn't know what they were up to now.

She played the recording. A female voice began speaking. "Niya saw the whole thing, you know what I'm sayin'? Niya was right there when Jay started shootin'. She really don't know her sister was fuckin' Tyriq. I know, 'cause I done seen text messages Jaz done sent to Tyriq, so I know what I'm talkin' about. I heard Jay talking about it and all that. Anyway, back to what I was sayin'—Jay found out Jaz was fuckin' Tyriq, and he was pissed off. I don't think he was mad enough to kill Jaz for that, though. After all, Jay fuckin' everything movin' anyway, but ... uh ... Jay took it to another level when his apartment got hit. He killed Tyriq for that shit and killed Jaz when he found out she was wit' Tyriq that same night. He swore Jaz had something to do wit' the move about that fifty Gs."

"How do you know that for sure?" a male voice asked.

Female voice: "I was fuckin' both of them, Jay and Tyriq, so I was down with everything that was goin' on. I was hip to it all. A lot of people don't know that when Jay gets drunk he talks a lot, more than he should. And he talks about shit he would never talk about if he wasn't drunk, you know what I'm sayin'?"

Male voice: "So you're telling me that Jay really killed Jasmine?"

Female voice: "Yeah, that's what I' m tellin' you. I couldn't believe it. That's when I knew his ass was crazy for real. I mean, I knew he wasn't to be fucked wit', but I didn't think he would really do some shit like that. That's some cold-blooded shit. He told me he was gon' do it, but I thought he was just talkin' 'cause he was drinking. He did that shit for real. The trip part about it, though, was he acted like that shit was nothin' to him. He didn't even lose no sleep behind it. Life went on like nothing had changed. I couldn't believe he was tryin' to look out for Niya like he really cared about her. Jay don't care about nobody but his damn self."

I couldn't believe my ears. I shook my head in disbelief and said, "I don't want to hear no more of this shit!"

"You need to hear it, you need to know who Jay really is," Phillips said.

Holmes hit a button on the device and said, "Listen to this, Niya."

Female voice: "Jay told me that if I ever told anybody about our conversation that he would kill me and wouldn't lose no sleep about it. I'm tellin' you, Jay's a cold muthafucka."

Male voice: "Again, how can you be sure Jay killed Jasmine?"

Female voice: "I'm tellin' you, Jay talks to me when he's drunk. He's one of those dudes that gets up close on their man, point-blank range shit. He got up so close on Jaz when he killed her that blood and brains and glass got all on his clothes and shit. He came to my apartment after the shit went down, told me to get rid of his clothes while he took a shower. Then he went back to the scene of the murder to see who was talkin' to the police. Shit, I heard he went over Niya's to see how she was doin', like he really gave a fuck. He even started takin' care of Niya after that shit. I know he was fuckin' her too."

Male voice: "Why would he go through all that to be close to Niya?"

Female voice: "Felt sorry for her. Her sister was all she had. Her mother's locked up, so she was fucked up in the game after that. I guess Jay wanted to look out for her or some shit like that."

There was a quick pause.

Male voice: "Why? Why are you giving us all this information?"

There was another pause.

Female voice: "I'm pissed off. Jay be on some bullshit. He act like he can do what he want to do. He ain't gon' carry me like that. He gon' cut me off and start fuckin' Niya? That's bullshit! After all the shit I did for that nigga, he gon' cut me off and start fuckin' Jaz's little sister? Then on top of that, I just found out I'm pregnant by this nigga. I can't stand that nigga no more."

My head was spinning. Tears were coming out of my eyes. My world was caving in on me. I didn't want to, but I began to believe what the detectives were saying: Jay murdered my sister.

I wiped away my tears. I was boiling with rage. My mind began racing, thinking of a way to have Jay murdered for what he had done. This muthafucka murdered my sister and was around me every fucking day like it wasn't shit to him. He even had me making moves for him. I felt dumb as shit. He was playing me every step of the way, and I was too blind to see it. He had me thinking another nigga killed my sister. I hated Jay, and I wanted him to suffer. Tish too. She knew all along he killed her. Shit, he told her he was gonna do it, so as far as I was concerned, she was down with the move, and she deserved to get dealt with too.

Detective Phillips cut the recorder off, leaned down to face me and said, "Don't protect Jay, Niya. Help us get his ass, help us put him away for all the dirt he's done, all the pain he's caused you. Do it for your sister, Niya."

I wiped away more tears, shaking my head in disbelief. Anger. Regret. Loss. Confusion. I felt it all at the same time. The pain of losing my sister was all back. I was the only one who was going to do something about what happened to Jaz.

"Do what's right , Niya," Detective Holmes said. "Tell us Jay killed Tyriq Brown, and we'll put him away for the rest of his life. He needs to pay for his wrongs."

Phillips added, "Come on, Niya, finger him as the shooter, and he's done for good, out for the count."

I took a deep breath, looked at both detectives and said, "I'm done here. I don't got shit else to say."

This Can't Be Life

Once the homicide detectives were done with me, I was sent to the dirty-ass D.C. Jail. Mentally and emotionally, I was a wreck. I kept it all inside, though. I didn't want to show any weakness. I wore my game face as I was processed, given a D.C. number, and sent to a cell block. It was late, and the cell block was dark and hot as shit. Everybody seemed to be asleep. I shook my head in disbelief as I was escorted to my cell. I was pissed that I had to spend the night there, but other issues took my mind off of that. All I could think about was my sister's murder and the fact that the muthafuckin' nigga who did it was right under my nose the whole time. Words couldn't describe my anger.

I was placed in a tiny, dirty-ass cell that would be my resting place for the night. No one was in the cell, so I had it to myself for the night. I needed to be alone to get my mind together. Just me and my thoughts. Without making up the bed, I took a seat and rubbed my hands through my hair and let out a long sigh. I shook my head, wondering what the fuck I was going to do next. I was damn sure going to do something. Jay was not going to get away with what he did to my sister.

I thought about how the detectives tried to use my sister's murder to get me to tell on Jay about Tyriq's murder. I was no fool, though if I was to tell the police I saw Jay smoke Tyriq, that would do nothing to make Jay pay for what he did to my sister. That would only get Jay locked up and charged with that murder, and while he was locked up for the murder, he would have somebody murder me since I was the only witness. After I was murdered, he would beat the murder charge and walk free. I wasn't going for that. I had to find a way to have Jay murdered in the streets. Fuck dealing with the court system. I wanted Jay dealt with in the streets. Plus I wasn't a rat, and I didn't want that title on my back.

As all kinds of thoughts raced through my head, I could hear Tish's voice saying, "I was fuckin' Jay too. ... He really did that shit. He killed Jasmine like it wasn't nothin' to him. ... I just found out I'm pregnant by him."

Tish had turned on Jay and was talking to the police. Hot-ass bitch. She was pregnant by Jay—or so she claimed—and she was trying to send him to prison for life. I couldn't believe what was going on. The shit was crazy.

I drifted off to sleep thinking about ways to make Jay's ass pay for he'd done.

* * *

The next day, I went to court and my case was no-papered, which meant I faced no charges. That was a blessing. I walked right out of the court building.

Outside, people were everywhere, coming and going. The heat was already baking the streets.

"Niya!" a voice called out.

I looked around and saw Face coming my way.

"I'm sorry about what happened. That's my bad for that shit that went down last night," Face said, grabbing both of my hands as he looked into my eyes.

"Don't trip. It ain't your fault, Face. I went off on my own. I just wasn't feelin' all that bullshit. I took it to another level. I should have let you deal wit' the shit, but them bitches pissed me off."

"You okay though?" He could tell there was something else wrong with me.

I shook my head. "Got a lot on my mind. It's nothin' really." I wasn't in the mood to let Face know what was really going on with me. I didn't want anyone to really know what was going on with me until I knew exactly what I planned to do.

Giving me an intense look, Face said, "Somethin' is wrong wit' you. You okay, for real? What's good? Talk to me."

I sighed. "Just a rough night. I'm okay. I just got a lot on my mind. Don't worry about me. Let's get out of here."

"Okay," he said, letting it go.

We jumped in a cab by the DC Bookdiva's Bookstand on 6th and Indiana Avenue and headed uptown. I was in a zone. My mind was racing. All I could think about was Jay killing my sister. Face put his arm around me and let me rest my head on his shoulder. I think he understood that I was going through something and that I needed to get my thoughts together on my own. I was pleased that he somewhat understood my situation.

As we rode up 7th Street in , Face told me they had no-papered his case as well. He was fucked up at Dena for all the bullshit that came with the night before. I was still fucked up about the whole situation. I wanted to see that bitch Dena, for real, but I had more pressing things on my mind. I would make it my business to see that bitch Dena in due time.

Face gave me a quick look and smirked.

"What?" I asked.

"You beat the shit outta that bitch last night."

I shook my head. That bitch asked for it, and I would have no problem giving it to her again. "Where them bitches from?"

"Dena from Landover, but she live out Temple Hills somewhere."

"Oh, yeah, I'ma see that bitch. I got cousins over that way."

Face smiled. "You vicious, like a female pit."

I shrugged.

"That was some wild shit last night." Face shook his head.

"Yeah, I know," I sighed, thinking about the news homicide had just dropped on me. Something clicked in my head, and I said, "I need to get my keys from the police station."

"Me too."

Face directed the cab driver to take us to the police station, where we got our belongings. Then we had the cab driver take us to Georgetown, where the Range was. It had a big, fat ticket on it, but at least it wasn't towed.

Face paid the cab driver, and we got out. I snatched the ticket off the truck and jumped inside. I unlocked the passenger's door and Face jumped in as well. We were on our way back uptown.

I couldn't have a real conversation with Face becausemy mind was still on my sister's murder.

"Niya, I can tell somethin' is really on your mind. Talk to me. Let me know what's going on."

I kept my eyes on the road. "Face, it's nothin'. I just have to get my thoughts together."

He sighed. I could tell he was frustrated that I wouldn't open up to him about what I was going through.

I couldn't open up to Face. There was no way I could let him know what I was really thinking. I had murder on my mind. I wanted Jay to pay with his life for what he'd done to my sister.

"Niya, I want you to know that I'm here for you, no matter what. Just know that."

That was good to know. "I know, Face. Thank you. Believe me."

For a moment, we didn't say a word.

I changed the subject and said, "So what you gon' do about that bitch Dena?"

"What you mean what I'm gon' do? What you talkin' about, the baby?"

"Yeah, she sayin' that's your baby. What you gon' do about it?"

"For real, Niya, I'm gon' do whatever I have to do to get her off my back. I don't want nothin' else to do with her ass after I get this blood test."

I nodded my head in agreement, then asked, "What if it's yours?" asked.

Face sighed. It was clear that he didn't want the conversation to move in that direction. "It's not mine, Niya, I'm tellin' you what I know. On everything I love."

"I believe you. I was just throwin' it out there. You deserve better that that bitch anyway."

"You right. That's why I want you. I ain't got time for all that bullshit." He leaned over and kissed me on the cheek.

"I like that. We'll work it out."

Face smiled.

* * *

I was at home sitting on my bed, wrapped in a towel. I had just taken a shower. I had so much on my mind I couldn't even think straight. I still didn't know how I was going to deal with the situation at hand. I had to play it cool until I figured out what I was gonna do. Until then, I needed to act like nothing was up. I knew that would be hard. I didn't know how I was going to act the next time I saw Jay. But I had to play my cards right, and that's exactly what I planned to do.

I rolled up some weed to try to clear my mind. I was stressing in a major way.

My cell phone rang, surprising me. I grabbed it and looked at the screen. It was Jay. Instantly, I became nervous. My hands trembled. I didn't know how to play the situation. My anger raced in the direction of rage. Fear joined the race as well. Jay was vicious. It was no telling how far he could go when he wanted someone dead. The phone rang a few more times, and I decided to answer.

"Hello," I said, my voice little shaky. I tried to hide how I was feeling, but it was hard.

"Niya, what's up wit' you? Where the hell you been? I been callin' you like shit." Jay sounded concerned and urgent.

I took a deep breath and placed the burning blunt in the ash tray. I knew I had to keep my cool and not let Jay catch on to the way I was feeling. To be honest, I was scared of Jay at this point. If he could kill Jaz like it was nothing to him, then I was sure he could do the same to me. That thought shook me to the core.

"I got locked up last night for some dumb shit."

"Locked up?! Locked up for what?!"

"I was out wit' a friend and this bitch jumped out there and disrespected me. I beat her ass, and the police showed up and locked everybody up. They no-papered the shit this morning. I just got in the house a little while ago."

"Oh, yeah? You okay?"

Like you give a fuck, nigga, I thought. He acted like he really cared. I hated him. I was burning with anger. I had to find a way to get his bitch ass for what he did to my sister. If it was the last thing I did, I was going to make sure his ass pay dearly.

"I'm okay, just a little tired. I'm 'bout to get some rest in a little while."

Just talking to him made my skin crawl.

"Ay, Niya, look, some serious shit is goin' down. I need you, baby girl."

I grew extremely uncomfortable. "What's up? What's wrong?"

"I don't want to rap over the phone. I'll put you on point when I see you. Grab them demonstrations you got left and meet me out Walker Mill. Cool?"

I wasn't ready to see Jay. I wasn't sure how I would act, and I didn't know what the fuck was going on with him. I didn't want to be alone with him at all. I had to find a way out of meeting him.

"I don't feel good right now. Can it wait?"

"Niya, did you hear what I just said? I need to see you as soon as possible. It's very important."

My heart began racing. I really couldn't tell Jay that I wasn't going to give him his bricks. He would surely nut up about that. I had to play it cool.

Reluctantly, I said, "Where at around Walker Mill?"

"In the back, by the school. Just hit me when you get there, and I'll come out. How long you gon' be?"

I took a deep breath and said, "I'm on my way now."

"Cool, just hit me when you get here."

I sat with my phone in my hand wondering what to do next. I was nervous as shit. My hands had started to tremble. I was not myself at all. Something told me to just say fuck Jay and not meet him at all, but I knew that was the wrong move. I needed him to feel like we were still on good terms. At least for the moment.

I got myself together and put my game face on. Shit was on another level now. I was going to play the game. Fuck it. In the end, Jay would pay for what he'd done. I was going to rock him to sleep.

A short while later, I was headed out of the door to meet Jay. I couldn't believe I was on my way to meet the muthafucka who murdered my sister. But I had to do it. I had to see everything through until the end if I wanted to come out on top. There was no way I was going to let this nigga win. He was fucking with the right one this time.

* * *

Carefully, I pulled up around Walker Mill and parked in the back, by the school. I saw a P.G. County police roll by. That made me nervous with all the coke I had in the truck with me. I watched the cop car leave the parking lot and turn left on Walker Mill Road. I felt a little better, but at the same time, I was ready to get the show on the road. I looked around and didn't see Jay anywhere. I pulled out my cell phone and called him.

"Yeah, where you at?" he answered.

"Out front, where you told me to meet you. Where you at?"

"Uhh ... I'm comin' now. But look here, I want you to leave out the parking lot, drive down the street, and then turn around and come back. Make sure you not bein' followed."

"Ain't nobody following me."

"Niya!" he snapped. "Just do it, please! I'll explain everything to you in a second."

I didn't say a word for a hot second. I didn't know what to think. He had never snapped on me like that before.

"Niya."

"I'm here."

"You heard what I said?"

"Yeah, I'm on it." I ended the call and started the truck. I looked around carefully and pulled out of the parking lot. I drove down the street, checking my rearview mirror. No one was following me as far as I could tell. I doubled back and parked in the same spot. Everything seemed cool. Moments later, my cell rang. It was Jay.

"Yeah," I answered.

"I'm comin' right now," he said, then hung up.

My heart began to race. I tried to calm myself, but on the real, I was nervous as shit.

A hot second later, I saw Jay coming my way. He wore a white T-shirt, blue jean shorts, and black Jordans. His hands were stuffed inside the pockets of his shorts. He was walking fast, like he was on a mission, which definitely didn't help me feel less nervous. All kinds of shit was going through my mind. I took a deep breath and told myself to chill out. Jay got in the passenger's seat and shut the door quickly. He looked around the parking lot suspiciously.

He had me spooked. He seemed highly paranoid. He seemed like he was backed into a corner with no options. Not a good sign at all.

I wish I had a gun on me. Looking at his muthafuckin' ass made me think about my sister. I could do it. I could kill him myself. But the time wasn't right, and on the real, I had no idea how to get away with killing his ass just yet. My thoughts weren't even clear. I just wanted to give him his coke and get the fuck away from him at the moment. He was acting strangely. I felt like he could read my mind. A sense of helplessness overcame me. I was alone with the nigga who killed my sister, and there was nothing I could do about it. I wasn't a killer. I didn't even own a gun. What could I do? How would I get it done and get away with it? Question after question ran through my mind.

"Ay, Niya," Jay said, taking another look around the parking lot.

The way he kept looking around the parking lot didn't help my nerves at all. I began to look around the parking lot in the same paranoid way. A terrible thought crossed my mind. Was Jay going to kill me? After all, I had seen him murder a nigga. He knew the police were pressing me for information about that murder. I was in a bad situation all the way around the board, but I had to play it out.

"I'm on the run, Niya. Feds ran up in my house looking for me. They hit my mother's house and my aunt's joint. They had homicide detectives wit' them and all that shit. I think it's about that Tyriq shit."

When I heard Tyriq's name come out of his mouth, my heart skipped a beat. I saw him smoke Tyriq. I was a living witness. I wanted to bolt out of the truck and take off running, but that wasn't an option. I knew how his mind worked. He had already thought about killing me. There was no getting around that. I began to question my decision to meet him alone. I thought I was playing shit cool by acting like nothing was up, but did he trick me to get me to come see him so he could kill me as well? Shit was fucked up.

"I gotta get out of town, Niya. I ain't goin' in for no murder. They got me fucked up."

A car pulled up behind us and slammed on the brakes abruptly. My heart skipped a beat. Jay whipped out his Glock and spun around, ready to get busy. I braced myself for gunfire.

The car behind us backed into a parking space two cars down from us. An old lady was driving it. I sighed and shook my head, relieved that nothing jumped off. I could tell that Jay was on edge. He was a loose fucking cannon.

Jay looked at me and said, "I gotta roll, Niya. Where that yay at?"

I handed him the backpack.

"Why your hands shaking like that? What's wrong?"

I hadn't even noticed that I was trembling.

"You actin' funny got me nervous, that's all."

He gave me an intense look. He was studying me, trying to read me as best as he could. It felt like he was reading my mind still, whicih made me uneasy. I began to study him as well, trying to read his body language. My eyes went from his eyes to the Glock in his hand and then back to his eyes. Everything inside of me told me to jump out of the truck and run, but I played it cool.

In a cold, calm voice, Jay said, "I trust you, Niya. You wouldn't cross me, would you?"

Like you crossed my sister, I thought. However, I said, "Cross you? Why would I cross you? You like family, Jay. Stop trippin'." I said that like I was surprised and offended at the same time. I had to play my cards right every step of the way. "Why would ask me some shit like that?"

"Just askin'. Shit is fucked up out here. I can't trust nobody. Can I trust you?"

"You know you can trust me. You've known me since I was little." My heart started pounding. I didn't feel safe alone with him. "Jay, I ain't no rat, and I would never cross you. Put it out of your mind."

He sighed and slightly shook his head like his stress level was on 1,000. His finger was rubbing the trigger of the Glock.

Looking me in the eyes, he said, "I trust you, Niya. I know you ain't no rat. I fucks wit' you. Always will."

His cell phone rang. He answered. Must have been bad news 'cause he ended the conversation quickly. With another sigh, he said, "Troy got locked up out P.G."

"For what?"

"His sister said it's a murder beef," Jay answered, looking around the parking lot, still on edge. "If it ain't one thing, it's another, I'm telling you. Then on top of that, I just got word that the nigga been talkin' to the police."

"No bullshit!?" I couldn't believe my ears. Jay and Troy had been through a rack of shit together. I couldn't believe Troy was a rat.

Jay shook his head in defeat. "You think you know these niggaz out here. But when shit hits the fan. … Niggaz got me fucked though, Niya. I'ma fix all this shit, and I'ma make niggaz pay dearly, even if it's the last thing I do in life."

Jay pulled a pack of Newports from his pocket and lit one. He hit that jack like it would be his last one. He was in deep thought. Blowing smoke in the air, he said, "I'm gon' need you to tie up a few loose ends for me. It will be some money in it for you, but right now you are the only one I can trust. Okay?"

"I got you. What you need me to do?"

"I got some money I need you to collect and bring to me. Can you handle that?"

"I got you. You know that."

"Good girl. I'ma call you when I'm ready, cool?"

"Okay."

"Cool, I'm gone." Jay got out of the car with the backpack and slid his pistol in his waistband. Before he shut the door he said, "Ay, Niya, remember that some things we gotta take to the grave wit' us."

I'm hip, I thought. I understood what he was getting at: Some things were never to be spoken about — ever! We all had to take certain things to the grave with us, certain dark secrets. If things worked out the way I wanted them to, he was going to wish that he went to his grave with the secret of killing my sister.

"You right, Jay. We gotta take some things to the grave with us. I feel you all the way."

<u>Fatal Thoughts</u>

Premeditation: To consider and plan beforehand. That's exactly what I was doing as I sat on the sofa in my living room watching "The F.B.I. Files" on Discovery. My mind was working nonstop. All I could think about was how I was going to get away with killing Jay. Nothing else was important to me at the time. I couldn't move on with my life until Jay was dealt with.

A whole week went by and I still hadn't put a move together to kill Jay, but that wasn't because I was plotting. I'd been thinking about it nonstop, but it was hard coming up with an unflawed plan. And there was no room for error because whatever I was going to do I planned to get away with it.

I was stressed out to say the least. I had too much on my mind. On top of having to deal with the Jay situation, I still had to find a way to get my moms out of prison. I pushed everything out of my mind and left the house. I headed downtown by the court building and went to check on a lawyer. I met with a lawyer who was supposed to be one of the best in D.C. We went over my mother's case. He assured me that he could help with the case, but I didn't get my hopes up too high. I was already hip to the fact that all lawyers talk that good shit to get your money. But I didn't give a fuck at this point. I had a few dollars stashed, and I needed to do something to help my moms. I dropped $5,000 on the lawyer and asked him to do whatever he had to do. I told him I would have some more paper for him as soon as the ball started rolling. That was that. With that in motion I was able to focus only on Jay.

I made it back home around 6:30 p.m. I took a shower and threw something on to lie around in. I needed to ease my mind. I rolled a Backwood of loud and drifted into thought. A knock on the door grabbed my attention. I looked through the peep hole. It was Bam.

"What's good?" I said as I opened the door.

"Ain't too much up right now, but shit 'bout to go down in a little while," he said as he walked over to the sofa and took a seat as I shut the door.

I looked at Bam's big ass and was glad to see him, glad that he was alive. His left arm was in a sling. Other than that he showed no signs of a nigga who had been shot in the chest a bunch of times. I felt bad that I hadn't made it to the hospital to see how Bam was doing, but I had so much going on in my life that I couldn't find the time to do much of anything. I had nothing but love for Bam, though, and he knew that.

"You don't even look like you got hit up like people sayin'." I walked over and took a seat beside Bam.

He lowered his eyes and shook his head like something sinister was on his mind. "I fucked up, Niya. I got Lil Quan killed. That shit was all my fault." He paused for a second as he thought about what he was saying. It was clear that he was hurt about what had happened to Lil Quan; the pain was all over his face and in his eyes. "On everything I love, I'ma tear Latif's ass up first chance I get."

I nodded. "I know how you feel, but that shit wasn't your fault. You ain't have no way of knowing how that shit was gon' play out. It could have been you that got killed, for real. Shit is fucked up. I'm hurt about what happened to Quan too, but I wouldn't blame you. I didn't want that shit to go down like that, though."

"I didn't want that shit to go down like that either, but it is what it is. I'm glad I had that vest on. I can't believe that bitch-ass nigga really made a move on us like that. I let him get the jump on us, but I got a cake baked for his ass," he said, shaking his head. "We was slippin', out there high as shit, bullshittin'." He pulled a .40-caliber Ruger from his waistband and set it on the coffee table. "I gotta put Latif in the dirt now. Ain't no way around it."

"I know how shit goes out here. Do what you gotta do, but don't get caught, Bam. Make sure you do it by yourself, and don't let nobody know what the deal is."

"No doubt, I feel you. I already know how it gotta be done, but right now I'm on some on sight shit, Niya. Wherever I see that nigga, it's going down, no questions asked."

There was nothing I could say to Bam, and I knew it. His mind was made up, and he was going to put his work in no matter what.

"Please be careful and think about whatever you do before you do it, Okay?"

He nodded. "I got you, Niya. I ain't gon' crash. I got this, but on another level, I need you in a big way."

"What's up? What you need?"

"I need to lay low for a second. Can you check me into a hotel under your name? The feds lookin' for me. You know I left the hospital early. I ain't even give them a chance to question me about the shootin'. On top of that, I had a vest on when they got on scene."

"That ain't nothin'. You family. I got you."

"Thanks, Niya. I fucks wit' you one hundred."

"You ain't even gotta say it. I'm always here for you, no matter what."

Bam gave me a look that told me my words meant a lot to him.

"Ay, Niya, don't let nobody know you seen me. I need to be a ghost to handle my business. I'm outnumbered for real. A lot of niggaz gon' pick sides wit' Latif, and I'm gon' deal wit' 'em all, on everything I love."

"Don't worry about that. You know I don't run my mouth. I got your back, Bam."

He nodded slowly as if he was thinking about his next move. "Niggaz gon' be fucked how I put this shit down. Shit gon' get real heated around here. Jay and them gon' be fucked up wit' me and all, but I don't give a fuck. Latif started this shit, so I'm gon' do what I gotta do to finish it. No questions asked. Feel me?"

"I feel you, but you don't have to worry about Jay. He got his hands full right now."

"What you mean?" Bam raised his eyebrows.

I told him that Jay was on the run and that Troy was locked up. I also told him that Jay said that Troy was talking to the feds. Bam was surprised to hear that Troy was telling.

Bam shook his head. "You never know these days. You think niggaz are real niggaz and then they do some shit like that. That's why I don't fuck wit' a bunch of niggaz out here. I ain't gon' give them a chance to cross me up like that. Fuck that shit. Niggaz ain't real no more."

A vicious thought crossed my mind. Bam loved me. He loved Jaz as well. He was my ace in the hole, exactly who I needed in my corner to take care of Jay. I was sure that once I put Bam on point about Jay and what he'd done to Jaz that Bam would have no problem smoking Jay for me. Plus I knew I could trust Bam. I was sure of that.

Bam could tell I was in deep thought. "What's wrong? What you thinkin' 'bout? You just drifted off into space on me."

"Bam, I gotta tell you something, but it can't leave this room, feel me? It gotta stay between me and you."

"Okay, what's up?"

"For real, Bam. If this shit gets out, it can cost me my life."

"Niya, what's the deal? Put me on point. What's wrong?"

I took a deep breath and got to the point. "Jay killed my sister."

Bam was speechless for a moment. Then he frowned and said, "Get the fuck outta here. Jay killed Jaz?!"

"On everything I love. That snake-ass nigga killed my sister and he walking around here like it ain't shit." I told Bam everything I knew, everything the detectives had said, leaving nothing out.

Bam was shocked. "Jay cruddy as shit. I woulda never thought he would do no shit like that." He shook his head like, Damn! "That nigga wrong as shit. You know what's up wit' me — I'll smoke that nigga. Just say the word. I know you want that nigga punished."

Bam reacted exactly as I thought he would. I had the right man for the job.

"I been wonderin' how I was gon' get his ass dealt wit', and then out of the blue you come knockin' at my door."

"Guess I'm right on time then. Where that nigga at?"

"I ain't exactly sure, for real. I think he out of town right now, but I'm gon' hear from him soon 'cause he need me to collect some money for him and take it to him. Soon as he calls, I'm gon' know where his ass at."

"Cool, I'm down. You already know that. I don't give a fuck about none of them niggaz. They don't fuck wit' me. Ain't none of them niggaz ever did shit for me when I was locked up. Fuck'em!"

"I feel you on that," I said.

"So you gon' Jay rocked to sleep, huh?"

"Yeah. And he don't even know I know he killed my sister. As far as I know, he think I'm out of the loop."

"Shit, we can smoke the nigga and keep the paper. I'm down wit' it, on everything. I already told you I don't give a fuck about none of them niggaz no more."

My cell phone rang. I didn't recognize the number on the screen but answered the call anyway.

"Yeah, hello."

"Niya, what's up? You busy?" a familiar voice asked.

"Who is this?"

"Troy. I need to holla at you."

I was caught off guard. I didn't expect to get a call from Troy, and being as though Jay told me that Troy was working with the feds, I really didn't want to talk to him. Nevertheless, I said, "Oh, what's up?"

"I'm locked up, and I can't catch up wit' Jay. I need you to tell him I said if he don't take care of this shit, he gon' be real fucked up when shit hit the fan."

"I ain't seen Jay in a couple days. I don't know where he at right now."

"Yeah, okay, well, when you see his ass, tell him I said I'm dead broke and my bond is five hundred thousand. I need him to touch my mother wit' that bread to get me out."

"As soon as I see him, I'm gon' tell him what you said."

"Thanks. Holla at you later." Troy hung up.

I sat my phone on the coffee table and shook my head. Troy was on some other shit, for real.

Bam looked at me and said, "What's good?"

"Troy talkin' 'bout he want Jay to pay his bond. His shit five hundredthousand."

"Damn. Ain't that some shit. Troy must think Jay don't know he tellin' — if that's true."

"You right," I said.

"Well, however shit go, if we get at Jay, we gotta get at Troy too, as far as I'm concerned."

I nodded. "You right. We'll figure it out."

* * *

I checked Bam into a hotel in Silver Spring, Maryland, and gave him a $1,000 to put some money in his pocket for a minute. He promised me he would lay low until it was time to make a move. He planned to go after Latif as soon as he got word on his whereabouts. Bam's mind was made up about what he was going to do to Latif, and I understood where he was coming from.

When I got back to my apartment, I began to plot. Jay was on borrowed time. If I had it my way, he would pay for what he did very soon. I wanted it over and done with so I could move on with my life as best as I could.

I rolled some weed to ease my mind. As my high set in, Face crossed my mind. I wanted to see him. I enjoyed being around him, but I just had too much on my mind to deal with anything other than the matter at hand. Besides, Face was down Atlanta trying to get his shit together with the music thing. The last text I got from him said that he was in the studio all night making things happen. I was pleased to hear that.

My cell rang. It was Face, calling as if he was thinking about me while I was thinking about him. I smiled when I saw his name light up the screen on my cell phone.

"Hello," I answered. I could hear music in the background.

"What's up, sexy? You okay up there?" Face asked.

"Yeah, I'm okay. Ain't too much going on. Just taking everything one day at a time," I said. I couldn't talk to him about what was really going on.

"I miss you. You need to come down here and chill wit' me. Shit is looking real good for a nigga down here. They got me in a sweet-ass hotel. I don't want for shit. They paying for everything. I got a little rental car to get around in, and I got a few dollars in my pocket."

"I'm glad things are working out for you. I wouldn't mind comin' down there. I have a few things to take care of up here wit' my mother's case. I got a lawyer on top of shit. Let me get all this shit straight, and I will be down there to see you. I can't wait to come down there and see you, okay, boo?"

"How long is that gon' take? A few days?"

"Not too long. I just need to make sure everything is in motion before I come down there."

"Sounds like a plan to me," he said. "That will give me a chance to make a few other moves I'm tryin' to make down here."

"Okay, that's a bet then."

Face and I spoke for a few more minutes and got off the phone with plans to hook up soon. I was looking forward to it, but I had one mission to see through first.

There was a knock at my door. I looked through the peep hole and couldn't believe my eyes. I opened the door.

Secrets Never Die

Bad move on my part.
I found myself looking down the barrel of a gun.

Life or Death

Terrified, my life flashed before my eyes. I had let death into my house. All I could think about was how I would die. I began to think of ways to get control of the situation; I knew my life depended on it.

"Where the fuck Bam at?" he hissed, grabbing my throat with a grip that was so tight it made my vision blur. I felt faint.

As I began to gag, I grabbed the nigga's hand and dug my nails into his skin. "I … I don't know! I don't know where the fuck he at!" I shouted, trying to snatch away, but this nigga was too strong. His grip around my throat began to tighten, and my knees got weak. I was close to blacking out.

The nigga kicked the door shut behind him and smacked the shit out of me with his pistol. I screamed out in pain.

"Shut up, bitch! You better tell me where Bam at right now or I'ma blow your fuckin' brains out! I already know he was here, so don't play dumb!"

I continued to struggle, trying to get his hands from around my throat. I couldn't breathe. I dropped to one knee. He smacked me in the face with the pistol again. This time he bust my lip. I wanted him dead. "I don't know where Bam at!"

He let me go and put the gun to my head while I tried to catch my breath. "Don't play, Niya. Don't make me kill you in this bitch, 'cause I will. Niggaz told me they saw him wit' you. This ain't about me and you, it's about Bam."

"I don't know, bitch!"

He smacked me with the gun again. I moaned in agony as I rolled around on the floor in pain. He kicked me in the side. It felt like he broke my ribs.

"I'ma ask you one more time, and then I'ma leave your brains all over this muthafuckin' floor!" He put the gun to my head again and cocked the hammer.

I could tell he was dead serious. Everything inside of me told me that he was going to kill me. Time was running out. I had to think fast, but what could I do? I wasn't giving up Bam; that was out of the question.

"Ok, ok, ok, Bam was here. I dropped him off at the Metro station. I don't know where he went, for real." Fear filled my voice. "I don't got shit to do wit' what y'all got goin' on, so don't put me wit' that shit!"

"You already wit' it, bitch! I should bus you right now!"

I squeezed my eyes shut and braced myself for what was to come next. I just knew he was about to pull the trigger and put a bullet in my head.

My cell phone rang. Latif's eyes darted in that direction. He eased over to the coffee table, still aiming the gun at me. He picked up my phone and looked at the screen.

"Who is this?" Latif said. "Where you at, slim? On the run?! I'm up in here lookin' for that young nigga, Bam. Niya actin' like she don't know where he at … What?! Nigga, fuck you mean nothin' bet' not happen to her?!"

I could tell it was Jay on the phone. His call was right on time.

Latif sighed, ended the call, and tossed the phone on the sofa. He gave me a long look, like he was contemplating my fate. The murderous end of his pistol was still glaring at me. I held my lip. I could taste blood in my mouth.

Latif walked toward me with a vicious look in his eyes. I want to scream and get up and run, but I couldn't make that move. Fear wouldn't let me. I closed my eyes as Latif got closer.

He lowered the gun and said, "You lucky Jay fucks wit' you so tough. I want to put a bullet in your head."

I still didn't open my eyes when he spoke. I just lay on the floor in pain, shaking with fear.

Seconds later, I heard footsteps. Then I heard my front door open and slam shut. Latif was gone.

Slowly, I opened my eyes. I was still trembling. Blood was running down my chin. I touched the blood and looked at it for second. Anger burned inside me. I couldn't believe this bitch-ass nigga had come inside my house and attacked me. Anger continued to burn my insides. It was more like rage, a rage that ran fear out of town.

"That muthafucka's gon' die!" I said.

I jumped to my feet and checked the door. I didn't open it, just made sure it was shut. I locked the door and put the chain on it. I had two muthafuckas on my shit list now. Latif was going to get what he had coming. I couldn't wait for Bam to catch up with his ass.

My cell phone rang again. It was Jay. \

"Yeah, hello!" I said with a serious attitude as I headed to the bathroom.

"Niya, you okay? What's up? You all right?" His tone was urgent.

It pissed me off to have to play this dumb-ass game with Jay. But I knew I had to if I wanted him to pay for what he did to my sister. I would give anything to see him pay with his life.

"Yeah, I'm okay for now, but that nigga Latif need his ass smoked! I thought he was going to kill me!" I looked in the mirror as I spoke. "That muthafucka bust my damn lip!"

"Where he at now?"

"He left!" I shouted Looking at my face sent my anger level up another notch. That bitch smacked me in the face wit' a fuckin' gun, Jay!"

"Don't worry about that nigga. I got his ass. Don't even trip. Trust me, he ain't gon' come back over there." Jay said that like he really cared about me.

I still couldn't believe how this nigga could murder my sister and then act like he really cared about me. He was a dangerous muthafucka.

"Ay, Niya, I need you to go pick up some bread for me right now. It's very important that you get right on top of this shit. I'ma' look out for you, trust me."

I sighed with frustration. "Where I got to go to get the money?"

"My man Dice gon' bring it to you. All you got to do is tell him where to meet you. He should be callin' you in a few minutes, okay?"

"Okay, I got it. Then what I do, bring you the paper? Where you at?"

"Yeah, I need you to bring me the paper. I'm in North Carolina right now."

"You want me to come all the way down North Carolina?!"

"Yeah, I got you. I'm gon' look out for you real good. Just call me after you meet Dice. Cool?"

I sighed. "Cool, I got you. As soon as your man call me, I'ma hit you right back and let you know what the deal is." I ended the call and began to clean my face up.

I had blood on my shirt. I went in my room and changed clothes. I looked out of the window and couldn't believe that Latif was standing across the street from my building like nothing was in the air. The nigga had to be out of his damn mind. The nigga was wanted for murder, and he had Bam on his ass. Having Bam on his ass was worse than having the feds on his back. The feds were trying to put his ass in prison; Bam was trying to put his ass in the dirt, and I was all for it. I rushed to get my cell phone and called Bam. I told him what had just happened and that Latif was still around the way, standing outside.

Bam said, "Ay, Niya, find a way to keep that nigga around there. I don't care what you have to do. I'm on my way right now!" Bam ended the call in a flash.

I ran back to the window to see if Latif was still outside. My mind was racing, trying to figure out what the hell I could do to keep Latif in the neighborhood. Terri was the first person that came to mind. I got her on the phone with the quickness.

I ran a quick idea by Terri and told her I would make sure I looked out for her with a few dollars. I just needed her to make a move for me real quick. She was down.

"Only because it's you, Niya. I'm on it!" she said.

I got off the phone with Terri and returned my attention to the window to watch Latif. He was standing out there running his damn mouth. Good! About two or three minutes later, Terri popped up. She came walking out of the alley, looking good as shit in her tight-ass boy shorts. She stepped to Latif and started a conversation. I had no idea what they were talking about. Terri could talk about anything. Everybody knew she knew what was going on in the streets, so there was no problem getting people to listen to her when she spoke.

I watched Terri pull Latif away from the two dudes he was talking to. They walked over to the fence and continued their conversation. It seemed like Latif was looking at Terri's ass more than looking her in the eyes as she spoke. It was all good, as far as I was concerned. I needed Terri to keep Latif's ass around the way as long as possible. I was sure Bam would pop up in a second, and when he did, I knew what he was going to do.

A few minutes passed. I was getting nervous. It was taking longer than I expected, but I knew Bam would show up. As I thought about that, I also thought about what Bam was coming to do when he got on the scene. Knowing Bam, he wasn't going to ask no questions; he was going to start shooting. I got on the phone and called Terri. She answered the phone in earshot of Latif, so I didn't want to say too much.

"Tell the nigga you gotta go, that you'll holla at him later. End the conversation."

Terri played it off good as shit. "Okay, Ma, I'm gon' run to the store and do that for you right now." She knew what she was doing.

I smiled and ended the call.

A short while later, I was letting Terri into my apartment.

"What the fuck happened to your face, Niya?" She looked very concerned, as a friend should.

"Latif was here. He smacked me in the face wit' his gun. He lookin' for Bam. He gon' find him real soon too. Watch!" I went on to explain the whole situation to her as I continued to watch Latif through the window.

"So Bam gon' smoke the nigga right now?"

"He on his way around here right now. Latif must think Bam hiding from him, but he not. He gon' tear his ass up."

"I know that's right." Terri went and took a seat on the sofa. "I can't believe that nigga Latif went like that on you. What he think Jay gon' say about that?"

"I don't know. Jay called while he was up in here. Whatever Jay said to him made him leave, so that's a blessing, but he still gon' get what he got comin'. Watch what I tell you."

I continued to look out of the widow. Latif was still posted up. I couldn't believe it. The nigga was out of his fuckin' mind.

"If Bam don't get Latif, I'm sure Jay will. He don't let shit go."

I didn't want to talk about Jay. I didn't even want Terri talking about him considering what I had planned for his ass. But I went with the flow.

"Yeah, Jay wasn't feelin' that shit when I talked to him. It is what it is, though. I ain't even trippin. Bam gon' take care of business, I'm tellin' you."

"Yeah, you right."

My cell phone rang. I looked down to see who was calling, and then gunshots went off. Sounded like fifteen or twenty shots, back to back. I dove on the floor. Terri did too. It sounded like the gunshots were right in my living room. More gunshots hit the air. Terri and I looked at one another and eased up at the same time. Carefully, we looked out the window and saw a masked gunman chasing Latif down the alley. He shot him in the back. We could tell it was Bam's big ass. Anybody who knew him could tell it was him. The mask did little to hide who he was.

Latif fell. Bam ran up, stood over him, and fired three more shots into his face. Flashes of fire spit from the barrel of the gun with every thunderous pop. Shells were flying everywhere   People outside were running scared. Nobody really wanted to be a witness to another murder around the way.

When the gun stopped firing, Bam took off running and disappeared around the corner. It all happened so fast. In a matter of seconds, Latif was a dead man. Just like that. I felt a funny feeling in my stomach, as if I was the one who pulled the trigger. However, the pain from where he'd smacked me with the pistol reminded me that I wanted him dead.

Terri put her hand over her mouth and said, "Oh, my God! Oh, my God! Bam punished his ass! Oh, my God! Did you see that shit, Niya?!"

Slowly, I turned my head to look at Terri and said, "No bullshit. He fucked him up real bad. That shit was like something out of a fuckin' movie."

"He got what he had comin' to him. That's what his ass get. What goes around comes around. I don't know what he thought was going to happen to him hangin' outside after what he did to you and Lil Quan."

Police sirens hit the air in no time—the station was right down the street. Police cars were coming from all directions.

"I can't watch no more," Terri said, then went and sat on the sofa again.

"You can't watch no more? You done seen it all now."

"You right," she said with a wink. "I'll take that to the grave wit' me."

I nodded. "That's right, take it to the grave wit' you."

Latif was gone, just like that. Jay was next.

It Goes Down

"Cash Money, Young Money, muthafuck the other side, they can fuck wit' me if they want, I bring 'em homicide," Bam rapped, spitting lines from the Lil Wayne CD that was pumping through the speakers of the Range as we headed around the beltway. He was carefully rolling a Backwood at the same time. He didn't even act like he had murdered a nigga earlier; it was nothing to him. That was wild to me, but I understood the code of the streets. Where we came from, it was an eye for an eye. It was in the Bible as well.

I looked into Bam's cold eyes as I drove. To be so young, he had the coldest eyes, like he'd been around forever and knew the ways of the world. After all he'd been through, I could understand why he was the way he was. The young nigga was heartless.

Lighting the Backwood, Bam took a long pull, held the smoke in his lungs with no problem, and said, "Did you see who was talkin' to the police after that shit went down?"

"John-John and Poo was the only ones talkin' to them peoples after that shit, but they ain't really see shit. They was in the carry-out, and the feds snatched them up just 'cause they was in the area. They couldn't tell the police nothin' if they wanted to."

Blowing smoke in the air as he nodded his head to the music, Bam said, "Man, them niggaz anything, when real niggaz start talkin' to the peoples? That shit crazy."

I shook my head at what he said as he passed me the Backwood. Bam was right. Street niggaz had no business talking to the police. "Don't trip off that shit," I said as I hit the Back. "Like I said, they ain't see shit no way. You was masked up. I mean, I knew it was you 'cause I know the frame of your body, but at the same time, nobody saw your face. We got bigger fish to fry anyway." I hit the Backwood a few more times and passed it back. "We gon' have to go out of town for a second anyway. That'll give you time to lay low for a second."

"Why we gotta go out of town?"

"I spoke to Jay before that shit went down wit' Latif. He want me to grab some money for him and take it to him down North Carolina somewhere. So that's where it's gon' go down, I think."

"Shit, that's cool wit' me. I can smoke that nigga down there, leave his ass there, and we can get right back on the highway." Bam nodded like he was thinking about the murder. "Yeah, I like the way that sounds. So when we gon' make that move?"

I shook my head. I had a young killer on the team. I was good.

My cell phone rang. The number was unavailable. I answered. It was my moms. A bunch of jailhouse noise was in the background.

"Hey, what's up?" I said.

"I'm okay. I'm holding on, taking it day for day. That's all I can do." My moms sounded like she was in good spirits.

"I know that's right. I'm gon' get you outta there real soon, believe that."

My moms laughed a little. "Niya, I told not to worry yourself about me. I'm doing all I can for myself."

"Ma, it's no way you can really think that I'm not gon' worry about you. That's not gon' happen. I need you out here. My life ain't complete without you out here wit' me."

"I understand, baby. I spoke to my lawyer today. He was talkin' real good too."

"Talkin' real good how? Put me on point!"

"Checked up on a few things and found out that one of my past convictions wasn't really a felony. It was really a misdemeanor, but somehow the paperwork was all twisted up and nobody told my lawyer after the mess was cleared up. You know how that goes. As soon as we fuck up, they all over our ass, but when they asses fuck up, it's a secret, and then when we get hip to the fuck up, all they do is say they sorry and they didn't mean nothin' by it. Bullshit! You meant something by it. That's why you sent my black ass away." She sighed. "Don't get me started. Anyway, the lawyer said he should be able to do something about it."

"That's cool. I sure hope so, but I still got you another lawyer anyway. I paid him some of the money and everything."

"Niya, I told you not to do that. You can't afford to be doin' that right now. You out there by yourself."

"Ma, I understand all that. I really do. But I'm a big girl now. I have to take care of myself, right? I know what I'm doing. Trust me!"

She sighed again. "Okay, Niya. Please be careful, no matter what you do. I really wish you would listen to me and stay out of this over here. I got myself in here, and I need to get myself out. As you said, I'm a big girl."

"Yeah you are, but I'm on your team, and no matter what I do in life, I want you to win. I want you to be out here and enjoying life with me. That's my main goal right now. I want you out of there, point blank."

"I understand, Niya. I understand. If I was you, I would do the same thing. Everything I ever did in life I did for my family. You got my blood in you."

"I sure do. Keep your head up. I'm gon' get you out of there."

We spoke about her case for a few more moments. It was eating me up that I couldn't talk to her about the Jay situation. I didn't want to worry her anyway, but even if I did want to talk to her, I knew I couldn't' get into it over the phone.

As if my mother was reading my mind, she said, "What's up with Jay? You seen him today?"

"No. He done got hisself in a little trouble and he ain't been around." I wanted my moms to think that Jay was out of the picture for a second. That way, I wouldn't have to explain so much once he turned up dead.

"I'm not even going to ask you why. I'm sure you'll tell me about it the next time I see you."

I nodded. "You right, Ma."

"I love you, Niya. I gotta go. Talk to you tomorrow, baby."

"Love you t—" The called ended before I could even get all of my words out. I hated those damn prison calls.

When I got off the phone, Bam said, "You gon' tell your mother about Jay?"

I shrugged. "I don't know. I think we need to keep all this shit between me and you right now. My moms don't need nothing else to worry about. She got enough on her mind, feel me?"

"I respect that." He passed me the Backwood. "It's all good by me. You ain't gotta worry about me sayin' shit to nobody. I know how to keep my mouth shut."

"I know, boo, that's why I fucks wit' you."

* * *

A short while later me and Bam were back at the hotel eating pizza. Weed smoke filled the air. The TV was on BET. I had just gotten off the phone with Jay's man Dice. We made plans to hook up around the corner from the hotel at the 7-Eleven. He said he would have everything that Jay asked for. I told him I'd meet him in about twenty minutes. That was a green light. Once that was done, the next part of the mission could go into effect.

My nerves were still a little jumpy from all that was going down, but I was good to go. I knew I had to do what I had to do. It was no turning back at this point—I was all in.

I looked at Bam and said, "I'm 'bout to go pick this money up real quick. Once I make this move, we can get the show on the road, feel me?"

"Yeah, I feel you. You want me to go get the money wit' you?" Bam asked, looking high as shit.

"Nah, I'm good. Just chill. I don't want the dude to see you wit' me. I don't need nothing gettin' back to Jay before we can make this happen, you know what I'm sayin'?"

"No doubt. That make all the sense in the world. Handle your business. I'll be here when you get back."

"Cool, see you when I get back."

I left the hotel with my mind racing. I took a deep breath and headed to the 7-Eleven. I parked and waited for Dice. Part of me wondered what was up with Dice. I didn't really know him. I looked around the parking lot to see if anything was out of place. Shit was cool. People were walking in and out of the store. Cars were at the gas pumps. Everything looked normal. Being in a public place made me feel at ease.

I looked through my rearview mirror and saw a dark blue Crown Vic enter the parking lot. It was Dice. My heart began to beat a little faster for some reason, but I stayed calm. Dice pulled up right beside me. I gave Dice a smile, got out of the Range, and headed for his car.

As I got in the Crown Vic, Dice said, "What's up, baby girl? You lookin' good as shit. I wish I could get to know you a little better, for real-for real."

I wasn't in the mode for flirting. I was trying to take care of business. "Maybe some other time. You got somethin' for me?"

Dice laughed. "That's right, let's get down to business. That's what's up." He handed me a black backpack. "Here you go."

The backpack had a nice weight to it. Dice lit a Newport and added, "That's a hundred stacks right there. Tell playboy I said I'm here if he need me for anything. I heard about the nigga Troy. That shit in the streets already."

"I'll let him know what you said as soon as I talk to him."

I got out of the car without another word. I jumped back in the Range and headed back to the hotel.

When I got back to the hotel, Bam was lying across the bed, smoked out. He was watching "Family Guy," laughing like shit. I just shook my head.

"You's a big-ass kid, boy."

"Nah, young, this joint funny as shit. You gotta listen to this wild-ass shit."

I tossed the backpack on the bed and said, "Check that out."

Bam stopped laughing and looked in the backpack. "Damn, that's a lot of paper right there. How much is it?"

"That's a hundred thousand. Half of it is yours, homie."

A huge smile spread across Bam's face. "Good lookin', Niya. Jay won't need it anyway, not when I'm done with him."

I smiled and shook my head. "Let's count it and make sure it's all there."

Bam dumped the money on the bed, and we began to count the paper. It took us no time at all.

Flipping through a stack of fifties, Bam said, "Damn, I'm jive sittin' nice right now. Fifty stacks gon' do me real nice. I'ma get me a lil' apartment, maybe one of them Chargers or a Camaro—something fast. You know? I ain't gon' look back. I'ma get me some work and start pumpin' like shit."

"Don't draw no tip on yourself. Be smooth wit' it. Don't even start spendin' no money 'til after this shit wit' Jay is over and done wit'. Feel me?"

"Yeah, Niya, I got you. You don't even have to say it twice."

"I don't want no attention to come our way wit' this shit," I said.

My cell phone rang a second later. It was Jay. I looked at Bam and said, "This Jay right here. Be quiet."

Bam gave me a quick nod.

"What's up?" I said.

"Everything went well wit' my man, right?" Jay asked.

"Yeah, it's all good." My heartbeat sped up. I still got nervous when I heard Jay's voice. I played it smooth, though. "I just seen him a hot second ago."

"You count that paper and make sure it's all there?"

"Yeah, I did that off the top. Everything is everything. You good."

"That's what's up, baby girl. I need you to do me one more favor."

"What's that?"

"I need you to go to the spot I took you to and get the paper out the safe for me. Cool?"

"I can do that." As far as I was concerned, that was more money for me and Bam to break down once Jay was dead.

Hegave me the combination to the safe. He said there was another $50,000 in there.

"How am I supposed to get inside? I don't have a key, Jay."

"That ain't nothin'. Just go to the rental office and tell 'em you my cousin and you need to get in the apartment. I'm gon' call 'em and let them know what's good."

"I can take care of all that. So when am I supposed to hook up wit' you?"

"As soon as possible. Tomorrow, if all goes well. I don't know how long I'm gon' stay down here. I might head down Atlanta. I got some peoples down there."

"Okay, so am I still meetin' you down North Carolina? Or somewhere else?"

"I'll let you know. Don't even worry about that, okay?"

"Okay, Jay. I got you!"

"Be lookin for my call, Niya. I might call you anytime, so I need you to be on point."

"I'm on it."

"Holla at you later."

"Cool."

"What's good?" Bam asked.

"Jay want me to pick up some more money from one of his apartments. After that, he gon' tell me where to meet him. Once he tell me to meet him somewhere, we can take care of business."

"Cool wit' me. I'm ready to get the shit over wit'. I know you are too."

"You damn right."

Bam stood up and said, "Let's get on it then. Ain't nothin' to it."

I grabbed my keys and we left.

* * *

The rental office didn't give me any problems about getting the keys to the apartment. Jay had gotten on top of that and made sure all was well.

Me and Bam entered the apartment carefully and began looking around. I headed for the bedroom. A funny feeling came over when I walked in Jay's bedroom. The last time I was in his bedroom we fucked the night away. Now I was in his bedroom to clean his fucking safe out like the IRS. I opened the safe, and there it was: $50,000. I smiled. There was also half a brick of hard white in there. Without a doubt, that was leaving with me as well.

Bam went through the apartment like the FBI. He was searching under the bed. I could tell by the way he was moving that he'd found something. He pulled out a black duffel bag.

While stuffing my backpack with stacks of money, I looked at Bam and said, "What's up? What's in the bag?"

"Heat." Bam held the bag open to reveal a bunch handguns and a box of bullets.

"I'm taking this shit too," Bam said as he zipped the bag up and threw it over his shoulder.

I shrugged; I didn't give a fuck. "Do you, homie."

Bam took a quick look at what I had taken out of the safe. He gave me an approving nod. "That's what's up."

"I'm hip. Now let's get outta here," I said as I finished stuffing the backpack with the contents of the safe.

"Yeah, you right, let's rock and roll up out this joint," Bam said, taking one last look around the apartment.

With what we'd come for in our possession, we headed for the door.

We jumped in the Range and took 295 to get back to D.C. I didn't want to play the streets of P.G. County too tough riding dirty. The freeway was always better, but I was still a little uneasy about all the shit we had on board.

I cut my eyes to the left and saw that Bam was lying back like it was just another day at the office.

He caught me looking at him and said, "You okay? You ain't in too deep, is you?" He smiled.

I sighed and shook my head. "No, I'm good, just thinkin' 'bout what's next."

"Jay is next. It ain't a whole lot to that. Bullshit ain't nothin'. He gon' get what he got comin'. Believe that, Niya. I don't give a fuck about him."

I nodded. I was listening to Bam, but I was also thinking about where we were going to stash the shit we'd taken from Jay's apartment. I didn't want the shit at my spot. For all I knew, the feds would be running up in my shit any day. And that's the last thing I needed with all I had going on.

"Where the hell can we stash this shit?" I asked.

"Shit, I don't know. I thought we could stash this shit at your spot," he answered, lighting a Capone.

"Nah, I don't want this shit at my spot. It's too much shit goin' on, you know what I mean? I mean, like, the feds done been to my door and shit. I don't need to have shit at my joint just in case they kick in my shit after this Jay shit go down. Feel me?"

Bam nodded. "Yeah, I feel you. We can always stash this shit over my grandmother's house. Ain't nothin' gon' happen to it over there. You wanna do that?"

That sounded good. Bam's grandmother lived on 14th Street, close to the Maryland line. We could stash the shit there for a second, at least the guns and drugs. I wanted to keep my money close. Anything could happen.

"Yeah, Bam, let's stash this shit over your people's joint for a hot second."

"You wanna do it right now?"

"Yeah, might as well get it out the way," I said.

We made our way to Bam's grandmother's house. I pulled into the dark alley and parked right behind her old white house. There was a light on in a room at the back of the house.

Bam looked at me and said, "I'm gon' put the straps and the yay in the house, cool?"

"Yeah, do that. We can keep the money wit' us for a second."

Bam gathered everything and got out of the truck.

I checked my text messages while he headed for the house. Face had sent me a text telling me that he was really feeling me. That made my day. I wished I had the time to focus on him. I sent him a quick text back and told him that I couldn't wait to come down Atlanta to see him. Terri had also sent me a text asking me if I was okay. I knew she was texting me because she hadn't seen me since Bam smoked Latif. I would call her later. I didn't really want to do too much talking over the phone anyway.

My mind drifted back to Jay. I couldn't wait to see the look on his face when he got what he had coming.

Bam returned to the truck in no time. He jumped inside and said, "I put that shit in the basement. My grandmother don't ever go down the basement."

I put the truck in reverse and said, "That's cool. We can come back and get the shit in a day or so, feel me?"

"Yeah, that's cool. So what we gon' do, lay at the hotel?"

"Yeah, we gon' do that until Jay calls. He should be calling in a little while. I know he needs that money right about now. He might call me in a little while. If so, we gon' go ahead and take care of his ass."

Bam smiled. "That's what's up." He lit the rest of the Backwood that he had left, which was a little less than a half. "I need some more smoke if we gon' be in the hotel all night."

I cut my eyes at Bam and said, "I'll get some smoke after I drop you off at the hotel. You don't need to be riding around right now."

"Cool wit' me. You might as well get us something to eat while you at it, Niya."

I shook my head and laughed. "You asking for a whole lot, ain't you?"

Bam smiled. "Come on, Niya, cut it out. You know I would do it for you."

"I got you, boy."

I dropped Bam off at the hotel and headed for the carry-out on Georgia Avenue to grab him a steak-n-cheese. I got me some chicken wings with mumbo sauce. I called my man Creek and told him to meet me on Rittenhouse Street so I could get Bam a pack of that loud. Creek met me within five minutes and hit me off with something nice. I headed right back to the hotel to call it a night.

Me and Bam smoked and ate our food while talking about Jay and what he'd done to Jaz. I really didn't like talking about it, but Bam just couldn't believe Jay had done some shit like that.

"I knew slim was a cold-blooded nigga, but I swore he loved Jaz," Bam said, lying on the bed, looking up at the ceiling. "I guess you never know a nigga until it's crunch time, huh?"

"Yeah, that's true, but Jay let his pride and emotions get to him on this shit here. He found out that old boy had hit him for that paper and thought that Jaz had something to do wit' it."

"Okay." I walked over to the window and looked out at the cars flying by. It had started to rain out of nowhere. I stood there for a second, deep in thought. I didn't know what the future held, but I felt as though I was ready for whatever. I could move on as soon as I put the whole Jay situation behind me for good. As I began to yawn, I realized that I needed to get some rest since I was going to have to get on the road to hook up with Jay.

* * *

It was almost 10 a.m. when my phone went off. It was Jay. My heart began to race when I saw his name on the screen. But I couldn't panic now; it was time to get the ball in motion. I took a quick look at Bam, who was knocked out cold beside me, and answered the phone.

"What's up, Jay? What's good?"

Bam woke up as soon as he heard me say Jay's name.

"Where you at, Niya?"

That question caught me off guard, for real. I wasn't ready to answer it. I said, "I'm over my cousin's house. Where you at?"

"I'm out Largo."

"Largo? I thought you was down South."

"I had to come back up here for a second. Had some unfinished business, feel me?"

"Yeah, I feel you," I said, wondering what his unfinished business was.

"Shit is wild out here, Niya. A nigga can't trust nobody, I'm telling you."

Tell me about it, nigga! I thought.

"You got that paper for me, right?"

"Yeah, I got you. Where you want to meet at?"

Jay was quiet for a second. I knew him. He was thinking about the safest place to meet me. Finally, he said, "Meet me at the uh … Largo Town Center. Cool?"

I didn't like that, but I didn't want to send off the wrong signal and let him know something was up. He felt like I was on his side, and that's just how I wanted him to feel.

"Yeah, how soon you want me there?" I said.

"Soon as possible, feel me? I'm on the clock, Niya." Jay was talking fast. I could tell he was still highly paranoid.

"I'm on my way. What you drivin'?" I asked.

"Don't worry about that. Just hit my phone when you get to Largo Town Center."

I took a deep breath, looked at Bam, and said, "It's game time, big boy."

"What's good?" He got up and took a long stretch. "Where the nigga at?"

"He want me to meet him out Largo Town Center as soon as possible."

I stood up and began pacing the floor. I didn't know what to do. How were we going to finish Jay out in public with hundreds of witnesses.

Bam raised his eyebrows and said, "How the fuck are we supposed to hit this nigga out Largo Town Center?"

I began to rub my temple, thinking hard and fast. I could only come up with one thing: "We gotta kidnap his ass."

"You right. That's the only thing we can do, but what if he has somebody wit' him? I might have to pop everybody."

I nodded. "I feel you. Let me think for a minute, Bam. Go ahead and wash your face and shit. I will come up with somethin'."

"Okay, cool, but trust and believe, I ain't got no problem poppin' everybody. That shit ain't nothin' to me," Bam said as he headed for the bathroom.

I began to run all kinds of things through my mind. I was the one calling the shots. Bam was willing to do anything I needed or wanted him to do. I knew he was down for whatever, but I wasn't going to send him out on a crash-dummy mission. I had too much love for him to let him go out like that. I could only think of two ways to play the situation. I could go ahead to the meet spot, get Bam to kidnap Jay, take him to another location, and then smoke him. Or I could play it all by ear and hope Jay would let me know where he was going. But I doubted he was gonna let anyone know where he was going, so I had to roll with my first idea.

Bam came out of the bathroom, wiping his face with a white washcloth. He said, "So what we gon' do, Niya?"

"We gon' have to snatch his ass, Bam. Can you do it without makin' a scene out there?" I folded my arms across my chest and waited for his answer.

Bam shrugged and said, "I can try, but I can't promise you nothin'. The nigga might buck. You know he stay strapped. If he buck, I'm gon' have to bus' his ass, and it might turn into an all-out shootout. You never know how the shit might go, feel me?"

I nodded in agreement. "You right." I gave the situation a little more thought. Shaking my head, I said, "Let's try to snatch his ass. I know you got my back. We gon' go 'head and roll wit' the shit."

"Cool, let's get this shit out the way." Bam grabbed his pistol off the nightstand and was ready to go.

* * *

It took me about twenty minutes to get to Largo Town Center. There weren't a lot of cars in the parking lot of the shopping center. That made me feel uneasy since I didn't know where Jay was. For all I knew, he was watching me pull into the parking lot. That made my stomach turn.

Bam could sense I was nervous. "You okay, Niya?" he asked.

"Just hoping this shit goes right. I can't let us get caught up out here."

"I feel you."

"Shit, I can't let Jay peep the move either."

"I got an idea, Niya."

"What's good?" I was open for whatever. I needed this shit to work, by any means.

"Pull over and park over there behind where the Sprint store at. I'll get out the car. Call the nigga and tell him something is wrong wit' the car. Tell the nigga the joint won't start. He gon' have to come to you that way, feel me?"

I thought about the move for a second. It was the best we could, so I was with it. "Let's do it."

"Cool."

"I'm not gon' let you out right here. I'm gon' pull up over there by the Metro and let you out. Just creep back this way as fast as you can. I'm gon' keep the nigga right here in the truck for as long as I can."

"Bet. That's what's up." Bam cocked the hammer on his pistol. I pulled out of the parking lot and dropped Bam off at the bus stop right outside of the subway station. In an effort to make things look normal, I drove all the way around the Metro station to get back to the parking lot in Largo Town Center. I parked between a Suburban and an old-ass Honda. It was game time. I was ready to get the shit over with, but I was nervous as shit. Fighting through my nervousness, I pulled out my phone and called Jay. The phone rang a few times. My heart beat faster with every ring.

"Yeah, what's good? Where you at?" Jay asked.

"I'm here, at Largo Town Center, behind the Sprint store."

"You in the Range, right? Never mind, I see you." He hung up.

Quickly, I looked around trying to see where Jay was coming from. I also looked around to see if I could see Bam from where I was parked. I didn't see either — not at first anyway. Like a ghost, Jay popped up at the passenger's window. The sight of his face in the window made me jump. He pulled on the handle of the door as if he was in a hurry to get inside. I hit the lock and let him inside.

"What's good, Niya?" Jay said as he looked around the parking lot.

"I'm okay." I was scared as shit. I knew that at any minute the whole move could turn sour and Jay could snap. It was a known fact that when Jay snapped somebody could end up dead. And I didn't want that somebody to be me.

"Where that shit at?" Jay said.

I reached into the back of the truck and grabbed the backpack, but before I could pull it off the floor, the passenger's door was snatched open with so much force it caused the truck to shake.

Bam grabbed Jay by the collar and jammed his pistol into Jay's face. My heart was racing. I couldn't believe it was really going down. Fear ran through my body. Just as I thought, Jay grabbed Bam's arm and forced his way out of the truck.

"You gon' have to kill me right here nigga!" Jay shouted as he and Bam slammed against the Suburban. Jay was much smaller than Bam, but he appeared to be stronger than he looked.

As they wrestled for the gun, Bam said, "I'm gon' kill you, nigga!"

All I could think about was Bam's pistol going off or the police riding by and seeing what was going on. I had to do something before Bam ended up firing the pistol. I jumped out of the truck and grabbed a crowbar from the back. In a flash, I dashed around the truck and smacked Jay in the back of the head with the crowbar. It felt like I cracked his head open. Jay went out like a light.

Bam aimed his pistol at his head for the kill but I pushed the gun away. "Not here, not right now. Get him in the truck!"

Bam grabbed Jay's limp body and threw him in the back seat and jumped in behind him. I slammed the door and ran around the truck to jump into the driver's seat. We needed to get out of dodge ASAP. I started the truck and tried my best to ease out of the parking lot without drawing any attention.

"Where we goin'?" Bam asked.

"I don't even know yet, but we gotta get out of here," I said as I headed toward P.G. Community College.

"I need to tie this nigga up until we get wherever the fuck we goin', Niya!"

Bam began snatching the shoestrings out of Jay's Gucci tennis shoes. In seconds, Bam had Jay's hands and feet tied up securely. He hog-tied the nigga. On point, Bam kept his pistol pointed at the back of Jay's head.

My mind was racing as I tried to figure out where the fuck I was going to take Jay. I wanted to dump his ass somewhere as soon as Bam popped him. I drove as carefully as possible, watching my rearview mirror like a hawk. My heart was pounding out of control. I stopped at a red light on Landover Road and stopped right beside a P.G. police cruiser. I couldn't believe my fucking luck.

The back windows on the truck were tinted, so I was sure the cop couldn't see what was going on in the back, but didn't ease my nerves at all!

"Just be easy, Niya. They ain't even payin' us no attention. Be easy!" Bam said.

"Okay."

I was trying not to look at the cop, but he just kept staring in my face. His stare was making me sweat, making me want to run the light just to get away from him.

The light turned green and I pulled off cautiously. The police cruiser turned off on Campus Way. I breathed a sigh of relief.

"Ay, Niya, you got a screwdriver in the back of the truck?"

"I don't know. I don't think so. Why?"

"'Cause if you do, I can steal a car out here and put this nigga in the trunk so we don't have to ride around like this. This shit is too hot. We askin' to get popped like this. Feel me?"

"You gotta check."

I made a left and pulled onto Kettering Drive. It was a nice neighborhood. Most people seemed to be at work in this part of town. I pulled over and parked under a huge tree at the end of the block.

With Jay still knocked out, Bam got out and jogged down the street. I watched him in the side mirror.

I was so nervous that my hands were shaking. As cars rode by, I tried not to make eye contact with anyone.

Jay began to moan groggily. *Oh my God!* He was coming back around. Panic rushed me like an attack dog.

"What the fuck is goin' on?" he asked in a low voice as he began to struggle to get free.

Anger was boiling inside me. "You know what the fuck is up, Jay. Don't act like you don't know what's up."

He continued to struggle. "Niya, you better untie me right now!"

"You think I don't know what you did? You think I don't know what you did to Jaz?"

"Untie me!" Jay shouted.

I turned around and looked at him. "You killed my sister, bitch, and I ain't gon' let you get away wit' it."

"You think you gon' get away wit' this?!" Jay yelled.

"I already got away wit' it. You got me fucked up, nigga!"

Jay went into a rage. He was twisting and turning, trying to get himself loose. He was making the whole truck shake.

A red Honda Accord pulled up right beside me, and my trunk was wide open. It spooked me for a second, until I saw Bam jumping out of the driver's seat.

I said, "This nigga is up!"

Jay was going off at this point, trying his best to get loose.

"So what?!" Bam said.

He snatched the back door open and smacked Jay with his pistol. "Shut the fuck up, nigga!"

Bam snatched Jay out of the Range and slammed him into the trunk of the Honda. "Let's get out of here right now," Bam said as he slammed the trunk shut.

Without waiting for me to respond, Bam jumped in the stolen car and pulled off. I followed him closely. He hit the beltway. He jumped in the fast lane and headed for Silver Spring, Maryland. There was a lot of traffic, but it was moving, so it didn't slow us down. I didn't like the idea of hitting the beltway, but there was nothing I could do about it. Bam was leading the way now. We pushed close to sixty-five miles an hour. We got off the beltway at the Georgia Avenue exit. Minutes later, we crossed the D.C. line and pulled into an alley. Bam turned into the lot of an abandoned garage. I stopped right behind him, wondering what was next. Bam came out of the garage and jogged up to my window.

"Drive around the block. I'll meet you at the corner in a hot second."

"Okay, hurry up," I said.

"I got you. Don't trip," he said and jogged back into the garage.

I pulled off and headed down the alley. When I pulled out onto the street, I parked at the end of the block. Moments later, I heard about three or four loud pops. I jumped at the sound of each pop. I looked around and saw Bam walking down the street like nothing happened. He got in the truck and winked at me.

"That's done. Let's get outta here, Niya."

No More Secrets

Bam didn't play no games with Jay. He shot him in the back of the head and then set the car on fire. I had nothing to say about that. Part of me wanted to see the look in Jay's eyes when he was dying, but on the real, I don't know if I could stomach that, so I was glad Bam did it the way he did it. I felt some kinda way about the whole thing, but everything inside of me told me that I was not wrong for what went down. The nigga killed my sister. I would never be the same after some shit like that. I would always mourn my sister. Nothing could bring her back.

After killing Jay, Bam and I went back to the hotel and chilled out for a while. I watched the news while we were there. The news reported that Troy had been bonded out of jail and was found dead the same day. It didn't take a rocket scientist to figure out what went down. Jay had come back to the D.C. area, got Troy out, and smoked him. He left him in the basement of an abandoned apartment building in Southeast. When I thought about it, I could have been one of Jay's victims if

I didn't play the cards I was dealt. In the end, I got his bitch ass and got away with the bread.

I wanted to leave D.C. for a while after the murder. Needed to clear my mind. I wanted Bam to leave the city too. We had money, so we hit the road. We headed to Atlanta. It was the best move I could have made. Face was on top of his business in the A. For three weeks, I stayed in a nice-ass hotel with Face and put everything about Jay out of my mind as best as I could. I got a number of phone calls from back home about Jay and Troy turning up dead. With no shame, I told everybody that I knew nothing about the situation. Terri knew it was a lie, but I didn't care. I had shut the door on a dark part of my past, and I never wanted to open that door again.

Bam loved it in Atlanta and planned to stay. That was a good move for him. He fit right in.

As much as I didn't want to go back home, I had to return to D.C. to tie up some loose ends. With the money I had, I packed up all of my shit and paid movers to take it to Atlanta, where I got myself an apartment. It was the first step in the process of starting my life over.

As weeks turned into months in Atlanta, Bam got his feet wet and found a sweet connect. He was getting pounds of weed for dirt cheap. That became his hustle, and he never looked back.

We were good. We had pulled it off.

Only one other matter had to be dealt with: my mother.

* * *

It was ice-cold outside as I sat at the bus station in Charleston, West Virginia. The heat inside my new black Porsche Cayenne Turbo was pumping. This was the day I had been waiting for. The day that seemed so far away from me at times. Between the lawyer I had paid and the lawyer my moms already had, her case was overturned. I couldn't believe it when I got the call that she was coming home. It all happened so fast. I had only been in Atlanta a little more than six months when I got the news.

Life was becoming normal again. Face was getting money producing. Bam was still Bam, although he had chilled out a little in Atlanta. He was more focused on getting money than dropping bodies, so that was a good thing. As for me, I took my little change and opened a store in the A. Of all the things I could have picked to sell, I chose books. I opened a book store called Down South Diva's Bookstore. I sold books, DVDs, and CDs, the basic shit that people came to get when they wanted some entertainment. I couldn't complain.

After Jay and Troy were found dead, the police put the press on me; they came all the way to Atlanta to fuck with me. I was worried for a minute, but my lawyer assured me that I had nothing to worry about. No witness, no crime. I was cool with that. They put the bite down a little harder on Bam. The feds knew that Bam was the one that smoked Latif; they just couldn't prove it. They still put a warrant out for his arrest and snatched him up. Once he was taken back to D.C., we found out that it was only for questioning. A few thousand dollars in the lawyer's hand took care of all of that. It seemed like we couldn't be touched. We had won. Out the corner of my eye, I saw my moms approaching my truck, carrying two bags. I couldn't believe it. She was free. I jumped out of the truck and ran toward her in the freezing cold. She dropped her bags and opened her arms to hug me.

"Ahhhhhhhhhhhhhhhhhhh!" I screamed as I squeezed her to death. "I can't believe it! I can't believe it! You are really here! You are really free!"

"Yes, but I'm gon' be dead if you don't stop squeezing me like that," she laughed. She couldn't stop smiling. "Let's get out of this cold-ass West Virginia air."

"Right."

We jumped back in the truck and headed for the highway. I couldn't stop looking at her—or smiling. I felt like if I stopped looking at her she would disappear and I would realize this was all a dream. But it wasn't. She was really here, sitting right next to me.

"You are really free!" I screamed. "I can't believe it! So how do you feel?"

With a huge smile on her face, she shrugged her shoulders and said, "I don't know how to feel. I know I feel good. I know I'm out here and not in there. The real feelings haven't set in yet. I'm just so happy to be free, to be sitting in this truck with you that I don't know what to do."

I nodded with a smile. "Put all of that behind you. It's a new day."

"You right."

She glanced out of the window and slipped into deep thought.

I left her to her thoughts. I knew she had a lot of mixed emotions after all she'd been through. I would feel the same way if I was in her shoes.

"You okay over there?" I asked.

"Yeah, I'm good. I'm okay. I was just thinking about Jaz. I wish she could have been here to see me walk out of prison."

I nodded. "I know. I feel the same way."

My mother and I had spoken about the whole situation with Jaz a number of times. I had put her on point about everything. At first, she couldn't believe what I had orchestrated, but after she gave it a little thought she admitted that she would have done the same thing, if not more.

"You know what, Niya? No matter how many times I thought about Jasmine and all that you told me happened, I could never see Jay hurting her. I just couldn't wrap my mind around it."

"My neither. I didn't want to believe it. I tried to make myself not believe it. But at the end of the day, I had to face the facts."

"You got that right. I don't know how Jay ever thought he was going to get away with that."

"He thought his secret was safe in the dark," I said

"Everything that's in the dark will always come to light."

"You can say that again."

My moms took a deep breath and said, "I will never know what was on Jay's mind when he did that to my baby, but whatever it was that's one secret that went to the grave with him."

"That'll hold 'em," I said, feeling no remorse for Jay.

My moms rubbed my head and said, "I love you girl. Always will. Jay got what he deserved. I guess that's now our little secret."

"Our secret for life."

About The Author

Eyone Williams was born and raised in Washington, D.C. He is a publisher (Fast Lane Entertainment), author, rapper and actor representing urban life in a way that is uniquely his. Known for hardcore, gritty novels, Eyone made the Don Diva best-seller list with his first novel, Fast Lane (Fast Lane Publications). He followed up his debut novel with Hell Razor Honeys 1 and 2 (Cartel Publications). He then delivered his readers a short story entitled The Cross (DC Bookdiva Publications) and Lorton Legends (DC Bookdiva Publications). He's also a staff writer for Don Diva Magazine , his most notable work is featured in Don Diva's issue 30, The Good, The Bad, and The Ugly, where he outlined the rise and fall of D.C. street legends Michael "Fray" Salters and Wayne Perry. Eyone's first acting role was in the forthcoming movie Dark City (District Hustle). His latest mixtape, A Killer'z Ambition, is a sound track to the novel, A Killer'z Ambition (DC Bookdiva Publications) by Nathan Welch.

For more information about Eyone Williams visit his Facebook page: facebook.com/eyone.williams

Order Form

DC Bookdiva Publications
#245 4401-A Connecticut Avenue, NW
Washington, DC 20008
dcbookdiva.com

Name: _____

Inmate ID: _____

Address: _____

City/State: _____ Zip: _____

QUANTITY	TITLES	PRICE	TOTAL
	Up The Way, Ben	15.00	
	Dynasty By Dutch	15.00	
	Dynasty 2 By Dutch	15.00	
	Trina, Darrell Debrew	15.00	
	A Killer'z Ambition, Nathan Welch	15.00	
	Lorton Legends, Eyone Williams	15.00	
	The Hustle	15.00	
	A Beautiful Satan	15.00	
	Secrets Never Die, Eyone Williams	15.00	

QUANTITY	TITLES	PRICE	TOTAL
	Coming Soon!		
	Q, Dutch	15.00	
	Dynasty 3	15.00	
	A Killer'z Ambition 2	15.00	
	A Beautiful Satan 2	15.00	

Sub-Total $_____

Shipping/Handling (Via US Media Mail) $3.95 1-2 Books, $7.95 1-3 Books, 4 or more titles-Free Shipping

Shipping $ _____ _____
Total Enclosed $_____

Certified or government issued checks and money orders, all mail in orders take 5-7 Business days to be delivered. Books can also be purchased on our website at dcbookdiva.com and by credit card at 1866-928-9990. Incarcerated readers receive 25% discount. Please pay $11.25 per book and apply the same shipping terms as stated above.